"Look at the baby, Mat. Go on, look. Remember Sam, and Lou, and Perce—"

"I remember. I remember."

"And I remember you, Mat."

Angrily, Mat jerked the rifle away. He aimed it down at the baby. The muzzle nudged the blanket-wrapped form.

"It's gotta be done."

"No. No, Mat—"

Hot on the trail of the murderous Lee Kincaid, Jubal Cade finds himself in the sleepy town of Rawson, Kansas—and smack in the middle of a bizarre feud. As guns blaze at him from all sides, he gradually unravels the tortured history of greed and betrayal, rape and lust, that locks a pathetic tribe of ragtag kids in mortal struggle with the powerful owner of the Hissing S ranch. But Jubal has his own irons in the fire—and his own BRAND OF VENGEANCE.

Also by Charles R. Pike

Jubal Cade / 11

Brand of Vengeance

Charles R. Pike

CHELSEA HOUSE
New York, London
1980

Chelsea House Publishers
Harold Steinberg, Chairman & Publisher
Andrew E. Norman, President
Susan Lusk, Vice President

A Division of Chelsea House Educational Communications, Inc.
133 Christopher Street, New York 10014

CHAPTER ONE

Jubal Cade rode his tired horse into Rawson just as the sun splashed lurid orange tints across the weathered boards of the town and lights began to flicker in the windows of the small outlying houses. The lamps in the saloons had been lit for half an hour or more and the batwings cut shadows across the dusty boardwalk.

Jubal could feel the tiredness in his bones. Rawson was more of a town than most in this territory and a man might hope to find a bath and a decent barber. That would be after he'd indulged himself in a full night's sleep in a real bed, the first in weeks, so he could relish the tiredness for a change instead of fighting it. Towns spelt trouble. Also, besides food and comfort, they spelt news.

Rawson began to open up for the night as Jubal let his horse carry him along the dusty main street. He aimed for the McEnery House, a weather-boarded hotel and saloon with a stoop whose wooden Indian showed more than a few bullet scars. But Jubal had no intention of riding any further than he had to, and the McEnery House would do.

The very normality of the town reassured him. He was so accustomed to sudden violence and death that the sight of a few late-hurrying men, the clip-clop of a team hauling a wagon out to the north where the road curved over a rickety bridge, even a handful of women pausing for a few last gossiping words, made him sink even further into a warm kind of contentment.

Here, in Rawson, so the red-headed man with the Bowie in his guts had said, he would find the scar-faced man.

When Jubal did at last catch up with the man with the four-inch scar furrowed across his forehead, the man with the insane laugh, he would kill him.

He still had not made up his mind if he would shoot him at

once, or if he would make him suffer first. Jubal Cade was no longer the same young man who had stepped ashore so eagerly in New York with his young bride Mary. Scarface had killed Mary. He had placed his Colt in her mouth and blasted the back of her head away. And Jubal had been through so much after that he doubted with a grim sadness that his beloved Mary would now recognize him.

He still wore his old grey derby, and the English suit, much mended and cleaned, and the old Spencer still jutted from the boot by his saddle.

The lights from the McEnery House beckoned warmly. The sounds of men drinking and laughing floated through the half-curtained windows. The higher shrieks of women as they pandered to the customers made Jubal's tight mouth curve downwards. Rawson was just another town. Here a man could find what he could pay for.

The blast of the shots battered from the doorway as Jubal reined in by the hitching rail.

The sound echoed over the town like a blatant challenge.

Before the echoes died Jubal slid from his pony, his Spencer in his hand, and crouched under the stoop, poised and watchful, like a wild animal attacked in its lair.

Jubal was not a big man but the man who appeared on the stoop was only an inch or so taller. Jubal stood just five feet six inches, slim and wiry with muscle; yet his size was deceptive, for he was large-boned and his tough frame was fleshed with hard muscular power. His face appeared young and easy-going, and when he smiled, which he often did, he shed several years; but when he frowned and his face took on the killing rage, then the full impact of his powerful personality could shock onlookers and drive them back in fear at the smouldering violence so clearly revealed.

The man dressed in the grey frock coat like Jubal's stood on the stoop with his hands half-raised, staring past the swinging doors through which he had been hurled by the force of the three bullets entering his body.

One slug had crunched through his chest, smashing a rib, ploughing on through flesh and sinew, splattering dark blood across his grey vest. The second bullet had gouged deep into his belly, bringing a slower-oozing redness to mingle with the first. The third wound centred between the first two, adding its quota of imminent death. Whoever had shot this man knew how to handle a gun.

But, whoever the gunman was, he was not satisfied.

As Jubal crouched in the orange-tinted shadows, the man on the stoop coughed blood and began to fall. The gunman shot again. This time the slug smashed into his jaw, splintering it, wrenching it sideways in a great splashing of bone shards and a gout of blood. The man fell. He toppled off the stoop backwards, his arms flailing and twisting, to crash into the street head first.

Jubal did not move.

Men were yelling. Women screamed and the sounds of tables and chairs overturning echoed from the saloon. The doors swung open.

A man stalked out. From Jubal's angle he looked immense – a great, towering, bear of a man. He spun a .44 Remington Army in an immense meaty hand thickly coated with coarse black hair and deftly slotted the gun into a quick-draw holster on a low-slung rig. He strode across to the figure in the dust and kicked him onto his back. The wounded man's thin arms flopped out. His mangled head rolled. The gunslinger spat confidently, hitched his gun-belt and swaggered off to a chest-nut stallion hitched to the rail over on the far side of the door.

He mounted up with an easy motion that told he could move fast despite his bulk. Jubal barely noticed him, remarking only the fancy checked shirt and dark vest, the denims, the silver-decorated Mexican boots, for his eyes were fixed on the face in the dust.

For a split second Jubal thought he was staring at himself, bloodily dying in the filth of the street.

The grey suit clothed a body not much bigger than his own. The watch chain draped across the ruined chest might have been twin to the Albert over Jubal's stomach. The man's face – what could be seen above the wreckage – was thin and seamed like Jubal's. The man was clearly dying. Only his hair was different, for he wore it a little long and it was a light chestnut touched with grey, whereas Jubal's hair was black and close-cropped.

No one was going to recover from wounds of that magnitude.

As the people of Rawson crowded out of the saloons and others ran across the street Jubal slowly stood up, letting the Spencer hang free.

'There a doctor in this town?' He spoke harshly. 'This feller's not dead yet.'

'Yeah. That's him.'

So the man in the dust not only resembled Jubal Cade, he was also, like Jubal, a doctor.

A stocky, fair-haired man pushed a red hand through his hair. He eyed Jubal suspiciously. 'Darndest thing. This big hairy fellow rides in, bellies up to th'bar, calls for a whiskey, sees the Doc come walking in, calls out "Doc" to him – and when Doc King turns around shoots him plumb through the vitals.'

'Yeah,' put in the barkeep, wiping his hands nervously on his striped apron, his face white and green in the shadows of the porch. 'Darndest thing. The hairy galoot shoots him again, twice. Doc's blown clean through the doors. It's crazy.'

A woman pushed through the crowd and with a sob flung herself down beside the dying man. She wore a decent grey dress with a poke-bonnet and so was not one of the saloon girls, who chattered and cried in back of the crowd and gaped fearfully from the balcony overhead.

'Henry! Henry—' The woman turned a tear-stained face up to the onlookers. 'Why'd anyone do it? What for?' She was not too old, about thirty, and Jubal judged she had not been married to Doctor King for very long. 'Do something! You can't just stand there.'

'Ain't nothin' to be done, Mrs King. The Doc's done fer.'

The woman did not believe him. Voices from the rear of the crowd lifted into the tight silence following the painful words. The voices carried no hint of the sorrow which gripped those closest to the dying doctor, only an absorbed interest in sensation.

8

'He shore c'd use an iron. He called out to Doc King and then drew. He shore was fast.'

'Yes, sir. Faster'n Kid Coley was, afore the Kid got his.'

'Reckon he c'd plug the Kid afore he'd cleared leather.'

'Remington Army it were. Nice lookin' piece.'

The woman's face glinted with sticky tear-streaks in the flickering light of the saloon as the crowd shifted and swayed. She implored them, her voice breaking.

'Help him, someone, please!' She stared desperately at the fair-haired man whose stocky body seemed to shrink beneath the gaze. 'Luke! Do something, for God's sake. Henry's hurting.'

The doctor in the dust could not groan; but a ghastly bubbling wheeze forced up past his shattered mouth. Mangled teeth fell. Blood dribbled down. He was suffering and could not scream out. His hands twisted and clenched. His feet thrashed. He looked a grotesque smashed puppet. Blood shone greasily on the front of his grey clothes, so much like the suit Jubal wore.

Jubal Cade had long passed the time when he would put himself out to assist anyone in danger. He had brought his bride, Mary, to the United States precisely in order to help those people in the expanding West who required the assistance of a doctor, a doctor trained in England who was a good man at his work. And the bloody viciousness of the New World had destroyed his wife and with her his feelings of compassion and compunction. The recent death of Andy, the blind young boy who had looked to Mary and himself as more than mere replacements for his dead parents, had completed that hard harshness of character. Now Jubal Cade believed himself to be a man dead to any desires that conflicted with the twin tasks he had set himself in life, tasks that would lead to death. His dream of being a doctor and working for the common good had been shattered. Shattered by men like the huge, bear-like gunslinger who had cut down Doctor King and left him to die in agony in the street.

Jubal looked again at the wounded doctor. The pain clawed at him, and he writhed, unable to shriek, making that horrific mewling sound. He twisted and his heels beat at the dirt. Jubal had seen that terrible reflex action before.

The doctor wore a white shirt and a black bootlace tie. The shirt was sparkling white where it was not fouled with blood. The end of the bootlace tie had been clipped by a slug from the Remington. Jubal's hand went to his own tie, and he knew how fouled and dirty his own shirt was. His grey derby, which looked oddly out of place in that gathering of Stetsons and slouch hats and wideawakes, he knew would be matched by this doctor's own derby. That would have rolled wildly away under the tables and chairs of the saloon as the first slugs smashed into Doctor King.

'Please!' implored Mrs King, her voice shaking, her hands fumbling together in a grotesque attitude of prayer.

For a moment Jubal saw Mary there, kneeling, imploring him to help ease the pain, as she would most certainly have done had she been there with him. He stepped to his horse and unstrapped his valise, thrusting the Spencer back into the boot. His movement brought Luke's suspicious gaze to centre on him. When Jubal put the black valise down in the dust beside the injured man, Mrs King burst out with a great sob of relief. Luke scowled.

'You a doc, then, too, stranger?'

Jubal did not answer directly. He snapped open the valise.

'I can ease Doctor King on his way.' He spoke harshly, feeling the futility of what he was doing; but unable to fight against the compulsion. He felt as though Mary stood at his elbow, encouraging him, urging him, with that sweet smile he remembered so well and still hungered for through the cold lonely nights.

A man thrust arrogantly through the crowd to stand straddle-legged before the dying doctor. He stood with his thumbs hooked over his belt, and his sagging belly bulging beneath his blue bib-fronted shirt. He wore his holster low, tied down. A silver star caught the last of the light and glittered on his chest.

He took in the scene with the raking glance that told him the whole story. Except for the stranger in the grey duds.

'You all see it happen?' He held up his hand at the chorus. He was more interested in Jubal. 'All right, all right. I'll hear it all.' He glared down on Jubal. 'You a doc, stranger?'

'Talking won't make any difference, Sheriff,' said Jubal, opening the valise. 'Just let me get on with my work.'

The sheriff had to make his presence felt. 'Ain't you better move Doc King inside? Get some light? It ain't decent for the doc to lie out in the street.'

'It won't make any difference.'

Mrs King emitted a choked sob and caught up one of the dying man's hands, pressing it between her breasts. Jubal took out a bottle and looked again at the dying man. Wrong. He looked at the dead man.

Without the flicker of an emotion on his face he put the bottle back in his valise, snapped it shut and started to buckle the straps.

'What are you doing!' demanded Mrs King, distraught. She started up, wild-eyed, her face hot, her pale brown hair falling from the bonnet about her burning cheeks. 'You must help him! You must!'

Before Jubal could frame a suitable reply that would not utterly crush her, the Sheriff spoke.

'Ain't no good nohow, Mrs King. Reckon the doc's dead.'

With a frenzied shriek the woman flung herself on the corpse. She hugged the dead man to herself, fouling her clothes with his blood. For a moment no one thought to move or say a thing.

Then Jubal stood up and backed off, heading towards his horse.

As though the movement broke the tension, the Sheriff started into action, asking his questions and getting a dozen shouted different answers. Two women appeared to take Mrs King away. They had to drag her from the body. Neither of the women could bear to look at the corpse's head. Mrs King's breasts shook under her bloodied bodice as she struggled with the women. Jubal turned away and began to buckle his valise back on his horse. He'd find a livery and bed the bay down and then take a room in the McEnery House.

The saloon and street crowd in Rawson had seen enough deaths for the spectacle to pall rapidly. Their extra excitement had been caused because it was Doc King who had been shot, and of the mysterious circumstances of the shooting. But now he was dead their interests shifted back to their normal pursuits.

Jubal watched the people moving back to the McEnery House and across the street to the other saloons. He finished up buckling his valise. A boy, young, scrawny, dressed in rags, his ankles and feet scratched and caked with dirt, squirmed his way past the horses hitched to the rail. He sidled up to Jubal, who half-turned, his hands still on the buckles of the valise. The butt of the Spencer carbine converted to a rifle firing .30 calibre bullets snouted up from the scabbard.

'You a real doc, mister?'

The boy's grimed face looked up with an intentness that Jubal forced himself to ignore. The boy was trembling.

'What's it to you, son?'

The youngster was about nine. Younger than Andy – but Andy was dead, killed a few months back, when Jubal had tried to rescue him from a kidnapper. The searing thoughts coruscating through Jubal's brain turned his face into a frozen mask of hate.

As the boy met that thin and bitter stare he took an involuntary step backwards. He swallowed down; but he came on in again, moving in closer, his hurried words spilling out breathlessly.

'It's my sister, doc. She's sick – real sick. Like for you to take a look at her.'

The words sounded strange, as though the boy hated to mouth them, only half-convinced of their truth. Jubal took his hands from the buckles.

'I'm not practising medicine in Rawson, son.'

'Please, doc.'

The words sounded more like a threat than a request. The boy's eyes stared at Jubal defiantly now, level and menacing. They were a man's eyes in a boy's face.

'She still bad tomorrow I'll take a look in the morning.' All the tiredness of the long ride hit Jubal in a wave of fatigue and near-dizziness. He rasped a hand over his stubbled chin. 'If I hadn't happened along she'd have had to take her chances.'

'Doc!'

With his left boot in the stirrup, Jubal started to swing up into the saddle. The sheriff looked across and yelled.

'Git away from decent folks, you Patterson trash!' He started across, his face red in the lamplight, his eyes glittering.

Jubal settled in the saddle and twitched the reins.

The boy cast a single venomous look at the sheriff and shouted a reply that was immediately lost in the sheriff's bellow of rage. All Jubal heard: 'Yore trash yourself, She'iff Lovesay—' The Sheriff's hand whipped to his holstered gun, and hovered. His face purpled. But he restrained his anger, and Jubal guessed that it would look bad for Lovesay's election prospects if he was seen to take a gun to a kid. The boy ducked away between the horses, which shied away at the smell of him.

Jubal heeled the horse into a slow walk to the livery, his body aching as though he had been chased across burning rock-strewn badlands by a war party of Comanche. He was just about all in. He needed rest.

A gaunt man wearing a tailor-made black cutaway coat and a black stovepipe hat banded with black ribbon, moved through the last of the crowd. He stood above the corpse and with a gesture of refined pleasure removed his hat. He held the be-ribboned stovepipe before his narrow stomach and looked down on all that was left of Doc King. His sparrow-like head tilted to one side.

Presently he clapped his hat back on, produced a tape measure from a tail pocket and bent to his work.

The iron lantern hanging on a weathered beam outside the livery shone more brightly as the sky darkened. One of the doors was fast shut, but Jubal guided his horse through the opening into the warm-smelling interior. A lamp shed a pool of light onto a straw- littered floor. At one side a small railed-off space showed a stool and table, and sets of harness hung on the wall. A big whisk broom half-concealed a pile of manure. The oldster who shuffled up, scratching under his armpits, looked cross and bitchy. His whiskery, leathery face did not soften at the sight of business.

'Danged kids! Creeping about in here like packrats. I'll whup 'em good when I catch 'em.'

He wore patched and faded denim overalls and his scalp was blotched with mustardy spots beneath his straggly white hairs. He pitched up a good gob of spit and let fly. He peered up with rheumy eyes at Jubal.

'Have to feed an' water him yorself, mister. Right through there. They's a lamp.'

'I'll be careful,' said Jubal, quite unnecessarily. But his fatigue was gaining on him now. He had to find a bed real soon. Any bed. He dismounted and paid the man, then led his horse past the first lamp. The bay moved now with a down-drooping head, as weary as his master.

The second lamp brightened the stabling area beyond a polished gig. The red-painted spokes, leather upholstery, and the air of care and attention, running even to a lick of gilding here and there, indicated that the gig belonged to someone well blessed with the hard necessities of life. Jubal blinked slowly and passed on, leading his horse, his mind focused completely on the speed with which he could feed and water the animal and then crawl into a bed.

He stopped stock still.

At the foot of a loose mass of hay tumbled from a feed box the small, blonde-haired figure lay exposed in the lamplight. She looked like a doll. She could not be much more than six years old, Jubal estimated, and her gingham dress, much torn and mended, had once been blue and white and was now scrubbed to a drab medium and dark grey. She moaned and moved a scabbad arm weakly, as though in pain.

The professional healing man in Jubal drove him forward. He guessed by the way she lay that she had crawled here to sleep off an injury, probably received in a savage beating by a drunken father. Her injuries could easily be far more serious than she supposed. The world held few more horrific surprises for a doctor out West.

He crossed the packed earth floor with its scattered covering of stray wisps of straw and hay in four strides.

He felt a brushing movement against his ankle and released his horse's reins, ready to bend to the girl. He felt a sudden constricting grip fasten like the jaws of a mountain lion around his ankle. The next second he felt the vicious yank at his leg, his feet flew from under him and he tumbled backwards. By his left ankle he was whipped up off the ground, the cunning rawhide loop gripping him securely as he dangled helplessly in the air.

His grey derby fell off and rolled away into the shadows.

He made a violent grab for the Colt; but it slid heavily from the shoulder holster and thudded onto the dirt. The lamplight whirled crazily about him. He was a good ten feet off the ground, spinning around and around, the blood beginning to roar in his ears. Upside down, yelling his head off, he spun about with the blood pounding crazily in his head.

Through his own involuntary yells he heard a low-pitched giggle followed by a sharp caution to silence. The doll-like girl on the hay leaped up, springing into galvanic life, and scooped up his Colt. The gun looked obscenely big and heavy in those frail hands.

'Put me down!' shouted Jubal. The pain in his ankle bit. His head whirled. The lamplight cut into his swimming eyes

'You the doc?' The voice was light; but it held a young and harsh authority Jubal recognized

'You know it! Let me down.'

'Allus do as a doc tells you. Best for you that way.' And the straining rope was abruptly released.

Jubal Cade pitched straight down onto the hard-packed dirt floor, crashing full on his head, feeling nothing and seeing only the darkness rushing in to envelop him.

CHAPTER TWO

Suffocating darkness pressed in on him from all sides.

His body stung with pain, a driving bite of agony around his head and ankle forcing out his fatigue. His mouth felt like those Apache-haunted badlands, burned and sucked dry and acrid with silica and dust. His head was enveloped in a sack. The gunny must have held dung at some time. He felt the stink invading every pore of his body.

He could just about breathe. His body with all its aches and pains was being jolted up and down in a familiar motion that told him he was in the bed of a wagon.

He'd been aching for a bed for the night; but this was not the kind he would have chosen for himself.

The grate of iron wheels on rock chips as the wagon swung off the trail told him exactly nothing. He had no idea where he was being taken, or who was taking him.

Something was making a regular noise, rhythmic banging, that eventually drove out his other worries. The metronomic thudding obsessed him. As the wagon rolled on, so that bang, bang, bang continued maddeningly. If someone was trying to drive him insane, they were going the right way about it.

He fought against the hypnotic effect. He tested the ropes binding his wrists and ankles again. When he strained his feet he felt the lash of pain circle his left ankle, and he let rip a gasp.

'The doc's awake, Mat.'

The voice was light, yet unmistakably it held a deeper note of resignation – and something else. Some other emotion in that young voice Jubal could not yet tag.

He tried to shout out and succeeded only in blowing an odoriferous mass of foul particles into his mouth and nostrils. He sneezed.

'You say something, doc?'

There followed a laugh, a low malicious giggle of rib-hugging enjoyment.

The grinding of wagon wheels continued. So did the monotonous banging, a sound that near drove him crazy trying to figure out what could be making the noise.

He spat and tried to speak again; but he knew even as he spoke the thick sack would muffle his voice.

'Lay quiet, doc. Soon be there.'

He'd pinpointed three voices. Three kids. So they were in the bed of the wagon with him. The guy driving the team would be the one to reckon with. Because there was nothing else he could do, Jubal forced himself to relax. He made his taut muscles loosen. He lay back and squirmed to find an easier position to ride out the wagon's jolts and lurches.

And all the time the bang, bang, bang continued like one of those diabolical Chinese tortures in English papers of his medical student days.

The grating of the iron-bound wheel rims changed to a softer slushing. The wagon creaked to a standstill and there was the muted sound of voices and the groaning of ancient timber. Then the wagon started up again and rolled on for perhaps fifty yards before finally coming to a stop.

In that moment the mysterious, infuriating banging stopped as well.

Hands grasped Jubal and pushed and tugged him towards the tailgate. He tried to help and a hand clouted him over the head.

'Lie easy, doc. We'll tell you when to use yore legs.'

Jubal tried to hawk up spit in the stinking gunny, and only croaked up dust.

His helpless body was swivelled around. He felt the edge of the tailgate cut agonizingly across his hip, then his legs were in mid air and being guided to the ground. He hit with a crash and almost toppled, but a multitude of hands held him up.

'Start walking, doc.'

Hooded, bound, helpless, Jubal was forced across the ground. His booted feet hit a stoop and he almost fell but again the many hands pushed and prodded and guided him. His ankles felt swollen and puffy after the ropes had been cut. He staggered again, reaching out helplessly with bound arms. All the hands that assisted him along touched his compact body low, around waist and thighs, and one pair even gave a succession of eager thrusts against his calves.

So how many kids were there in this kidnap gang?

They jabbered among each other, but the movement and the muffling sack prevented Jubal from hearing more than occasional snatches of what was said. He gathered the ringleader was called Mat, and there was a Perce and a Sam and a Lou. He could hear no sound to indicate the man driving the rig had stepped down to join the kids.

His boots hit boards. They creaked. He staggered forward, felt an anxious hand jerk him sideways, and cannoned off a doorpost. His legs gave out around then and he fell full length. No one offered to support him any longer and so he guessed he'd arrived.

To prove it, he felt a knife at the gunny's strings.

'Careful, Sam. Don't want the doc's gizzard slit afore he looks at Beth.'

'I ain't a baby any more, Mat, so you quit ridin' me.'

Jubal felt almost sure the one called Sam was the urchin who had accosted him outside the McEnery House after Doc King had been shot. If it was, then some sense could be discerned in this farce.

The foul-smelling sack was whipped from his head and brilliant light shafted in.

The particles of dung loosened from the stinking fibres of the sack had stung his eyes and sent an almost irresistible urge to rub them thrilling through his body. Had his hands not been bound he would have had to fight that urge to claw at his stinging eyes. Moisture welled and the whole world turned into a scarlet haze. He clamped his eyelids shut and the pain struck.

'Stand up, doc, so's we kin see you.'

Jubal made no attempt to stand. He lay there, suffering, his face a mask of agony.

A foot thudded into his ribs.

It was a small foot, bare-toed, and a furious, high-pitched voice screamed: 'Stan' up when Mat tells yuh!'

'Stand up when I'm good and ready,' Jubal ground out. His jaws were stiff. He sounded like an old water wheel turning in the first rain after the Flood.

A hand gripped the back of his grey coat. But its owner did not have the strength to hoist the five feet six of Jubal Cade to his feet. Jubal was small, but his bones were thick and clothed with compact masses of muscle. He rolled over, breaking the hand's grip on his shoulder.

The scarlet whorls settled down. By an effort of will power he forced himself to study the gang who had kidnapped him.

Kids. Just kids. The one called Sam was the one who had beseeched him to attend to his sick sister. Lou aimed a bare-toed kick at Jubal as he lay there. Jubal saw the thin, scratched shanks, the dirty feet, the faded gingham dress. Lou had suckered him beautifully in the livery. She'd set him up perfectly. The snagging rope had looped him like a coney. He stared at Lou with an expression that drove her back. Yet he forced the blazing anger from him, felt the skin slacken from its tautness over his high cheekbones. If these kids had kidnapped him, it could only mean they were serious about their sick sister, Beth.

Perce must be the kid about ten or eleven with the shock of fair hair and the ripped denims through which his skin showed grey and pocked. He grinned all the time, not with an imbecile's grin, but darn close. Now he sat on a rickety table and kicked his bare feet against the leg. Bang, bang, bang.

Suddenly Jubal realized the source of that mysterious, infuriating sound in the wagon. All the way from Rawson out here, Perce had sat banging his heel against the side of the wagon. Without knowing it, he had devised a subtle torture for Jubal that had almost worked.

Forcing his attention away from the swinging filthy foot of Perce, Jubal studied Mat. He was around fourteen, big and yet not filled out as he ought to be, and Jubal could quite clearly see the tell-tale marks of malnutrition. They were all thin and hungry. These kids were down to the starvation line.

'Any more of you?'

Mat smiled, displaying yellow teeth.

'Surely. There's Zack out bringing in yore gear. We got yore valise, doc, cause you're gonna need it real soon.'

Jubal sat up, fighting the dizziness. His tiredness remained with him; but now he thought he understood a little of what was going on and the first fears had ebbed, he found that he could relish the situation.

A gang of unwashed verminous kids, kidnapping a doctor to attend to their sick sister!

If Jubal cared about such things, this would be a story he wouldn't want to spread around.

'Can't do much with my hands tied.'

Mat turned to Sam.

'Go get the rifle, Sam.'

Solemnly, they waited for Sam to return. Jubal took the time to study the room. Just a wooden shack interior, with a rickety table, wobbly chairs, a stove and a dresser with pots and pans in disarray. It was mostly broken down stuff, the impedimenta of a poor family making out against indifferent fate. He noticed the stove was burning fiercely, and the four big pots set atop it were bubbling, the steam rising and cooling.

So they knew that much, then.

He eyed Mat calmly.

'When's she due, son? Do you know?'

'About now, I reckon.'

'Can't hear anything.'

'She's all right. You'll see soon enough.'

Lou looked up sharply, wiping a drip from her nose.

'You oughtta've let me help Kath—'

'Hesh up, Lou, now.'

The child sniffed and then wandered across to the double bunks against the far wall and rummaged under a mess of crumpled blankets. She found what she was looking for and came back to stand staring fixedly at Jubal. In her scrawny arms she cradled a doll made from old material stuffed with straw, with buttons for eyes, and a right leg much chewed.

Jubal looked away.

On the wall beside the single grimy window a cheap farmer's

calendar had been pinned up. The date was out by two years. Alongside it and striking an incongruous note in the room was pinned a coloured picture cut from a magazine. The colouring was amateur and lurid, and done, Jubal guessed, by one of the children. The picture showed a handsome-looking man in Confederate grey, with sweeping moustaches and wearing an officer's hat, grey, very fancy, with an exaggerated curling brim and a rakish feather. The yellow collar, cuffs and belt buckle still glowed with some of its original enthusiasm. Whoever had coloured the picture had wanted to show a Confederate cavalry captain, the doubled Austrian knots reaching well up past the elbows of the uniform sleeves.

In a photographer's chair at the captain's side sat a woman wearing good plain clothes of a severe cut, but showing traces of elegance and fashion. Her face had been so coloured over that it was unrecognizable.

Mat saw the direction of Jubal's stare.

He shook his head.

'Naw,' he said. 'Kath cut it outta a book a carpetbagger left, years ago. She coloured it up real purty.'

Jubal stored the information away.

Sam came back with the rifle.

Jubal, despite his predicament, despite the tiredness and the pains in him, had to stifle the beginnings of a laugh.

Old as it was, antiquated as it was, the rifle could blow a massive hole through his guts.

Sam struggled in with it, holding it up manfully with both hands, and Mat took it from him.

Mat pointed the long barrel at Jubal and hauled back on the hammer. The rifle was an Enfield, model 1853, a rifle-musket, percussion, not adapted for breech-loading, and Jubal fancied Mat knew how to use it. He had learned to shoot as Jubal himself had once learned, the hard way, shooting time after time and hitting nothing, being blown onto his backside, until he had mastered the gun.

Back at the orphanage in Chicago, young Jubal Cade and his friend had stumbled across a Nathan Starr flintlock in the basement, and there they had practised until they could shoot, as

21

Jubal put it, better'n anyone else in Chicago. The friend had been killed in one of the last engagements of the War Between the States, and had left his Spencer repeater to his friend. With a rifle, there was little anyone could teach Jubal Cade.

'Cut him free, Sam.' Mat jerked the rifle-musket's barrel meaningfully. 'I c'n knock the eye off a fly at twenty paces. So remember that, doc.'

'I believe you, son.'

Jubal drew his cramped wrists before his body as the confining ropes fell away. The onrushing return of blood made him clamp his teeth together and he massaged his wrists, looking up at Mat. A choked cry sounded from the inner room.

'Hadn't we better be getting on with it?'

'When you're ready. Git your hands working, first.'

Jubal nodded. Whoever he might be, this Mat, for all his scraggy appearance and his air of dirt and malnutrition, knew his own mind. The girl, Beth, was the person really in command of the timing. Jubal stood up, conscious of the black muzzle of the Enfield and walked across to the stove. He poured water and waited a space for it to come off the boil – no one was going to plunge their hands into boiling water for anything less than the kind of reason pointing at him now.

Zack came in with the valise. Zack was clearly a brother, shabby and hungry like them all, with a bitter twist to his lips made all the more sinister – and pathetic – by the youthfulness of his pallid features. If the leader Mat was around fourteen and Perce was ten, then Zack slotted between them. He was around eleven or twelve.

'Don't look much for a doc, do he?' greeted Zack.

Mat jerked the rifle-musket muzzle.

'Check the valise, doc. Make sure you got it all there.'

'Hey! Mat,' said Zack. His bitter lips twisted in a grin of wolfish enjoyment. 'So you c'n go boil yore haid!'

'Doc,' said Mat, a little pompous in his words and manner. 'Brother Zack c'n steal yore shoes off'n yore feet even if you was dancing in St Louis. Ain't no one like him.'

Snapping the valise open, Jubal nodded, checking through the contents. So that explained a little of how this Patterson family managed to scrape some kind of living. He guessed the farm would be pretty much run down. His medical equipment and supplies were untouched. He looked up.

'Take a look at Beth now, Mat.'

'Reckon so.'

'Need to wash my hands.'

The kids stared at him.

'You just washed.' Mat indicated by his manner he had little truck with washing as a general rule of life.

'Touched the valise since.'

'So?'

Jubal decided the time for fun and games was over – if any such time had ever existed. He was confident that if he tried anything stupid with these trigger-happy kids he'd be blasted through the door with a damned great hole in him.

'Let's get started.'

The far end of the ramshackle farmhouse had been burned. Recently, Jubal judged. Less than a year. The wood's blackened surface still showed the brittle gleam of charred wood-grain. The roof had been patched. When it rained the roof would leak like a sieve. A corner of the far room had been boarded up in better style and a blanket draped a broken doorway. Mat pushed through and turned, the Enfield centred on Jubal. Sam held the blanket. Jubal stepped through.

At least there was a proper bed.

It was of cast iron, had once been ornate, with brass knobs, and was now covered in bedclothes that shone with a strange cleanliness in that decrepit shack. The girl in the bed lay quietly, breathing shallowly, the bulge of her stomach clearly visible beneath the bedclothes. Jubal's eyes jerked to the woman sitting in the bentwood rocker in the corner.

She looked as though the world had run over her and flattened her into the ground, indifferent to her and her sufferings. Her grey hair was scraped back to leave a lined forehead bare. Her eyes looked out dully from the wreckage of a face that had once been more than ordinarily beautiful. Her slack body rested in the rocker as though exhausted after too much toil; the grey shapeless dress was patched and stained. Her hands were like claws, veinous, hooked, as they gripped the twelve bore, its twin muzzles centred directly on Jubal's heart.

'All right, Ma,' said Mat quickly. 'It's the doc.'

The woman rocked back, the scuffed runners squealing on the bare wooden floor. The shotgun moved up and then down as she rocked back. But in all its rocking movement the shotgun remained aimed firmly on Jubal.

'The doc? That ain't Doc King. You foolin' me, Mat?'

'Doc King got shot. This here's a new doc.'

Again the woman rocked back and forth.

'Didn't reckon Doc King'd come out here anyhow. Where'd you find this one?'

Through the rough careless speech of the territory, Jubal caught echoes of a more refined speech as though once, long ago, this shattered woman had once known a gentler life.

'He was just there. He looks like a dude, don't he?'

The faded eyes regarded Jubal gravely. 'I am pleased to make your acquaintance, young man. I hope you are a good doctor. My daughter Beth needs expert assistance.' The shotgun did not waver from Jubal's heart.

'Pleased to meet you, ma'am,' said Jubal, fully aware of the strangeness of the situation and the conversation. He went to the bed and put his valise on a broken crate at the side. He stared down on the girl. Abruptly her face contorted. She let out a wild shriek, writhing, fighting the pain, then as suddenly relaxed, letting out a long shuddering moan. Sweat shone greasily along her forehead and Jubal gently wiped it away.

Although it was difficult to judge, Jubal placed her age at around seventeen. Young. He had now made the acquaintance of or heard about seven children ... There could easily be others. As a doctor he had heard other doctors raging against this incessant child-bearing that dragged women down, made them old before their time. But Mrs Patterson had been wrecked by other forces besides child-birth.

Was her daughter to follow the same life?

Jubal cleared his throat.

He had to ask the question, and yet he was uneasily aware the answer could hold danger for him.

'Is the father around?' he asked, easily, beginning to lift the bedclothes.

'He ain't,' snapped Mat.

'You need not concern yourself over the whereabouts of the father,' said Mrs Patterson. 'Just deliver my daughter.'

Bending over, still wearing the derby the kids had given him back, his hand on the bedclothes, Jubal said: 'I'll do all I can, Mrs Patterson.'

'You don't,' said a voice from his back – Jubal thought it would be Zack's voice – 'you get a hide shot full of lead.'

'Where's Kath?' demanded Mat, suddenly, looking about.

'Her leg hurt her,' said Mrs Patterson. The rocking of the chair ceased. 'She went out for a spell.'

'Get her back!' yelled Mat. He waved the Enfield wrathfully. 'Sam! Go on and find Kath.'

'Goin', Mat,' said Sam. He sounded scared. He ran out like a chased coney.

It would not take much to make Mat squeeze that trigger.

The arrangements were primitive and not of the best. The boiling water was too far away. But Jubal prepared carefully, pushing the tiredness from him. His head still ached from the crack his skull had taken falling from the beam when he'd been hog-tied by these kids. His ankle still stung. His body was a mass of aches and pains. But he forced them all away and concentrated on what he had been trained to do. Seven years he had spent in England, learning medicine, thinking that, perhaps, he might one day call himself a real doctor. He had found a wife. And then it had all gone smash.

This would have been a great part of his life if Mary had not been killed. His dedication to finding and killing her murderer had not dimmed. It remained with him, scarlet and demanding, afresh every day. But, with a girl waiting to bear a child before him, needing his skill, Jubal felt very sure that Mary would want, would demand, that he do all he could for Beth.

He had reached bitter decisions about himself. He was a man who, trained as a doctor, had become a killer. And he knew too that killing was easy for him. His every dream had been destroyed. Perhaps he might salve a little back now . . .

A noise at the blanket-covered doorway made him turn.

Footfalls approached, strange, hesitant footfalls, a firm thud of a shoe against the boarded floor and then a scraping, dragging sound, and then the firm thump again. There was a world of labour and suffering in that tortured gait.

Beth in the bed moaned and rolled her head from side to side. Her hands clenched.

The contractions were coming on her now. Jubal turned back to his task. He had taken off his derby, his jacket, and rolled up his shirt sleeves. The waters would come down soon. Beth would be quick, he felt sure; but there was always that odd nasty chance of complications.

'Lou,' he said. 'Fetch cold water. Bathe her forehead.'

Mrs Patterson rocked forward.

'I'll send the kids out in good time,' said Jubal.

The limping footsteps paused at the blanket and a white hand pushed the folds of cloth up in a weary gesture. Lou strutted out importantly, bent on her mission.

'You boys can git out now,' said Jubal. He spoke firmly. 'This is women's and doctor's work.'

'I'm staying, doc,' said Mat. The Enfield underlined his meaning.

The blanket fell into place after Lou. Jubal straightened and turned.

The girl who entered looked wan and ground down, her light brown hair bedraggled and in a tangle about her shoulders. Her grey dress hung from bony shoulders. She looked to be about sixteen, and yet in that pallid face shone the burgeoning beauty that had once been her mother's. She limped forward, staring at Jubal.

'Time you got here, Kath,' said Mat, crossly.

Jubal stared at Kath, seeing at once and with a savage pang that she resembled in an uncanny way his dead wife Mary. But Mary had never looked so beaten, so disheartened, as this girl.

She carried a pot of hot water. She came forward with her thud, scrape, thud, scrape, dragging her left foot. Her left hip jutted awkwardly under the grey dress. Every step was a labour.

She halted before Jubal.

'Are you a good doctor?' she said, in a low, simple voice. 'Can you help Beth and the baby?'

'I'll do all I can,' said Jubal. 'Just recently, I've got more used to helping people out of this life than into it.'

CHAPTER THREE

The baby was born along towards six the next morning. It was a boy. The birth had not been as easy as Jubal had expected. Although Beth was young, her frailty did not help. Also there was something else, a puzzling lack of enthusiasm, something more than the usual fear of the unknown faced by any woman at the birth of her firstborn.

Jubal sat stupidly on a broken crate as Kath wrapped the baby in clothes put by. Although he'd lifted the mite up by the heels, all gleaming and red, ready to give it the smack to bring air to its lungs, that had not been necessary. The baby had yelled lustily almost at once, so its raw red bottom remained unsmacked.

He felt as though his head would roll forward and fall off. But there was more to do yet. He rose and moved to the bed, bending down over Beth, whose pale face, gleaming with fresh sweat, rolled against the damp pillow.

Very gently, Jubal unlaced the strings of her white nightgown and pulled the frayed edges down. He half-turned to Kath. 'Here, Kath. Bring the baby.'

Carefully, he eased Beth to a sitting position and bunched the pillows. He drew her nightdress down exposing her left breast. It shone, engorged, small but plump, the nipple hard and erect and swollen.

'There won't be any milk yet,' he told Kath. 'But if the baby sucks it will help with the afterbirth.' He let Kath place the baby tenderly into the crook of Beth's arm. 'And any mother has a right to hold her firstborn the moment he's born.'

Then Jubal stared in stupefaction as Beth turned her head away, laboriously, refusing to look on her baby. She let her crooked arm fall. The baby bawled. Her breast shone, full and plump and inviting, but she would not hold the baby's sucking mouth to her nipple.

'Go on, Beth. It won't hurt – at least, not much at first, and then – well, I'm told it's a most wonderful sensation for a woman to suckle her baby.'

'No,' Beth gasped the words. Her hair shone with sweat. 'No – I won't. Take it away! Take it away!'

Kath snatched the child away, cradling it, holding it to her own bosom. Jubal nodded. Cases like this were known – in fact, for the very first time they were not all that unusual. But again, strongly, he sensed the strangeness of this particular birth. Beth moaned again, and turned herself in the bed, slipping down, her mouth opening, her eyes closing.

'Let her sleep, I guess,' said Jubal.

All the time Mrs Patterson sat in her rocker, rocking backwards and forwards, the shotgun in her lap, the muzzle pointed, her finger alongside the twin triggers.

All the kids except Mat had fallen asleep and were snoring and snuffling in the main room of the shack. Mat had placed the Enfield in the corner by his mother. He sat on the floor, head back, arms folded, fighting sleep.

'It's a fine boy, Mrs Patterson,' said Jubal, wiping his hands.

The woman merely rocked back and forth, back and forth. But at Jubal's words her clawlike finger curled towards the triggers, and she raised the ugly snout of the twelve bore.

'Mebbe,' she said in a rough, choked voice.

Kath had slept a little during the night on Jubal's instructions. Now he tried to force a smile at her. Despite his convictions that he would have no truck with other people's problems, he had been sucked into the drama of this poverty-stricken family. He had been practising the kind of medicine he should have been doing if Mary had not been killed. It gave him a strange sensation. Occasionally he could see some pattern to his life; usually he could see only darkness and storm and a desperate emptiness and grief.

'You need some sleep, doctor,' Kath's pallid face gleamed in the lamplight as she glanced across at Beth, who moaned and moved her head slightly but remained asleep. 'Beth is all right for a spell, I guess.'

'You know what to do?'

'Surely.'

'Call me if—'

'We'll call you, doc,' said Mrs Patterson. The grimness of her words was not lost on Jubal.

He stretched out on the floor with a threadbare blanket and was instantly asleep.

A choked gurgle broke from Mat's throat. His head snapped forward. He blinked and shook his head and spat, clearing the spittle that had choked him out of a light doze. He peered around the shack's inner room blearily. Lamplight blotched the walls and glittered off the charred beams.

Kath smiled at her brother, holding the baby cradled in her arms, swaddled against the hostile world.

'It's a boy all right, Mat.'

'Yeah?'

Kath looked down on the tiny, pink, crumpled face, and she sighed. The baby looked like – like – she couldn't quite think what the baby reminded her of. When young Lou had been born she had felt just the same, only different. She'd been Perce's age then, of course.

The family cradle had been positioned ready. Its ancient wood, much polished, revealed cracks and the prominences of knots. But it was still sound. It had served the Patterson family well. From the big cast-iron bed to the wooden cradle was but a short space in the Patterson family, as in so very many families of the time.

Mat stood up and picked up the Enfield. The baby slept peacefully and Kath knew there was no need to feed him yet. Later, when Beth's milk came, they might have trouble with the new mother.

The folds of cloth were laid just so by Kath. She straightened up, half-smiling, wondering if ever she would have a baby and dreading and welcoming the awesome experience to come.

She turned and looked full into the black muzzle of the rifle.

'Mat! What—?'

'Step aside, Kath. Rest easy.' Mat was sweating. His dirty knuckles showed yellow as he gripped the rifle-musket. 'I guess you know.'

'But—'

'We fetched the doc for Beth, didn't we? Sure. Not fer the baby.'

Kath swallowed. She could feel her heart thundering away in her breast. She felt faint. And her damned stupid horrible bent leg pained her, as though the winter was coming on.

'Mat!'

The boy almost at manhood pushed forward. He thrust the rifle down, pointing the muzzle at the sleeping baby. The cold steel nudged the tiny form. Kath put the back of her hand to her mouth. Her eyes grew round and wide and her chest felt as though it would explode.

'Mat!'

'Filth,' Mat said. He was panting. 'Ain't gonna let it live in this house.'

'You can't, Mat! Ma will tell us—

'Ma's asleep.'

Kath swung her paining body about, aiming to hobble to her mother. The rifle switched up, catching Kath across the belly.

'No, Kath. Let Ma sleep. She ain't had a good sleep for too long – I know – you know, too.'

'But, the baby, Mat! You can't—'

Holding the rifle barrel against his sister, Mat stared down on the baby. A frown creased between his eyebrows. The rifle shook – not much, just a little – but Kath felt that betraying tremor and a wild hope leaped in her.

'Look at the baby, Mat. Go on, look. Remember Sam, and Lou, and Perce—'

'I remember. I remember.'

'And I remember you, Mat.'

Angrily, Mat jerked the rifle away. He aimed it down at the baby. The muzzle nudged the blanket-wrapped form.

'It's gotta be done.'

'No. No, Mat—'

The rifle trembled. Sweat beaded on Mat's forehead. His eyes hurt. He felt the stock of the rifle in his hands, the chill of the trigger against his finger. Just a little pull, a little pressure, and a life would be snuffed out. It would not be difficult. And it was a thing that had to be done, must be done—

'Mat! No – please!'

Between them there was no need to express the emotions that tormented them. They knew. Mat glared at the baby and Kath stared at her brother with anguished eyes.

The rifle jerked as Mat could not control the quiver that set his muscles trembling. The muzzle nudged into the baby.

The baby opened its mouth and yelled.

The cry, weak at first, grew, filling the tiny room with the sound that nature designed to demand instant attention, a sound that cannot be disregarded save at enormous cost. Mat's sweat dripped past the corner of his eye, and he let the rifle go with one hand to dash a fist across his face. The baby yelled on.

Mat seized the rifle again, pointed it firmly at the baby.

'Gotta be done. Gotta do it,' he ground out.

His finger tightened on the trigger – tightened and fell away.

In that instant Kath felt the certainty that her brother despite his words and feelings could not do what he had threatened.

The tableau remained. Kath, pallid-faced, flinching back, gazing with horror on Mat, who held the rifle jammed into the crying body of the baby, his face desperate, sweating, his eyes glaring madly.

A pair of strong, sinewy hands took the rifle away from Mat as though twitching a straw-stalk from a field.

'Guess that's the wrong kind of nourishment for the baby,' said Jubal.

He stood, half-crouched, the rifle reversed and pointing at Mat's belly.

'Doc!'

'Take care of my patients, Mat. Pride myself on that.'

Mat's young face, old before its time, crumpled.

'It shouldn't be let live! It's gotta die!'

'Plenty of chance of that, without your help, son.'

Kath took her hand away from her face.

'What are you going to do, doctor? Don't kill Mat—'

'Why not?'

'Cause iffen you do I'll blow your insides all over the room, doc,' said Mrs Patterson, grimly.

Jubal whirled. The woman sat forward in the rocker, the shotgun a twin-barrelled menace, hard and firm, aimed at his belly.

Gently, Jubal lowered the hammer.

He held the rifle muzzle up. He eyed Mrs Patterson.

She sat awkwardly, as far forward as she could get, and her ravaged face showed that she would shoot given the slightest reason to do so.

'Can't say I like the idea of a lady holding a gun on me, ma'am,' said Jubal.

The woman's tones changed as she said: 'One has to learn to accept many unpleasant things in life, doctor, as you must surely know.'

Jubal nodded. He looked carefully at Kath. 'See to the baby, Kath?'

At least, that gave the crippled girl something to do.

Mat stood, dejected, eyeing his rifle, ready to snatch it the moment he felt safe to do so. Mrs Patterson, for all that she was chained to her rocking chair, dominated the family in moments of crisis like this. Now the middle-aged woman jerked the shotgun at Mat.

'Git your rifle, son. And then git out. Catch up on some sleep. I'll think on about the baby.'

'Yes, Ma,' said Mat. He snatched the rifle and, with an eloquent look at Jubal, went out.

Jubal let out a little sigh.

'Going to tell me about it, Mrs Patterson?'

'Not your business, doc.'

'Guessed you'd say that.'

The baby quietened down, for Kath had had plenty of experience. She tucked the baby back into the cradle, her pale fingers like moths in the lamplight.

'He likely to have another try?' said Jubal.

'Not if I say no,' said Mrs Patterson. Jubal believed her. Her power of command, despite her immobility, did not come from the shotgun in her clawed hands.

'The hand that rocks the cradle,' said Jubal.

Kath stared at him anxiously. 'You need your sleep, doctor.'

'Needing and getting don't necessarily always meet up, Kath. Think I'll stay awake a spell. You go get some sleep.' Jubal turned away from the crippled girl, again seeing that heart-breaking likeness to Mary. He stared levelly at Mrs Patterson. 'Do I get to leaving in the morning?'

'Your work is finished here. We thank you for it. Mat'll arrange it for you – in the morning.'

'Won't be long, now. Sun's almost up.'

'Anxious to be gone?'

'Anxious to be doing what I came to Rawson to do.'

Mrs Patterson eased her shapeless body back into the rocking-chair. The twelve bore remained levelled. Her face showed not the slightest interest in Jubal's words. She didn't want to know what he'd come to Rawson to do. She was totally immersed in the problems of her family.

Jubal could understand that.

Shortly after that Jubal was busy once more as a doctor, and he carried out his professional duties without fuss. Kath, aroused from a fitful sleep, proved of tremendous help. Her quiet, sensible presence sustained Jubal as he had once fondly imagined his wife Mary would sustain him in his planned life as a Western doctor.

Beth lay washed out and exhausted. She was weak, but Jubal had no more than the usual fears for her. If the fever took her, the fever would take her. Puerperal fever was a killer, had always been a killer, and would remain a killer. One day, perhaps, the doctors would discover means of really arresting the ghastly effects. The Europeans were working on it. Jubal stretched tiredly and Kath glanced across at him.

'You really ought to get some rest.'

'And the baby?'

'Ma'll look out for him.'

'Mat—'

She crinkled up her small nose. 'He's a man – well, almost a man. Men are turned off by babies and childbirth. It frightens them.'

34

'True. But that doesn't explain—'

'Leave it, Doctor Cade! It's family business.'

Only then did Jubal realize he was becoming more involved than he liked with this Patterson family. He had delivered the daughter of a baby son; his work was over and he should leave. But he still considered the problem of Mat's attitude merited further probing.

Kath would have none of it.

She shooed him out to the other room. All the kids were out and away, about the chores and foraging no doubt. From outside came the sound of an axe biting into wood. Of breakfast there was no sign.

Zack came in with a bucket of water. He smiled when he saw Kath and sucked in his cheeks as he transferred his gaze from his sister to Jubal.

'All right, son. You got my horse?'

Zack nodded and giggled.

'Sure enough. Easy. Old Seth at the livery never knowed a thing.'

'You know what they do to hoss thieves?'

'Gotta catch 'em first.'

Jubal shook his head. This family lived close to the danger line as well as on the starvation line. But they were of no concern to him. His mission in life was to seek out the killer of his wife and, at the same time, to escape the hired guns sent after him by Ben Agnew, who dearly wanted him dead.

He cocked his head. 'You hear any more about the shooting of Doc King when you were in Rawson, Zack?'

'Nope. Big hairy guy waited for the Doc, shot him, and rode off. That's all.'

Jubal knew very well that that was not all.

'Anybody know this hairy guy?'

'Nope.'

Again Jubal gave the young horse thief a close look. If anybody would know, Zack might. So, with little hope, Jubal said: 'Ever run across a fellow with a scar? Big guy, handsome, you might say, with eyes dark enough to be near black. Handles twin Colts real mean. Scar about four inches long across his forehead.'

Before he had finished speaking he saw by Zack's face that the youngster knew something.

Jubal stepped forward and gripped Zack's elbow. His thin fierce fingers dug in and the boy let out a squeak of pain.

'Tell me, Zack! You know.'

'Sure, doc, sure. I know. Lee – that's him, gotta be. Lee. He rides with the Croxley boys.' The bitter twist to Zack's lips became more pronounced. 'If I'd hadda gun I'd'a shot the whole bunch.'

Jubal stepped back. He swayed with fatigue and reaction.

So the red-headed man, dying with a knife in his guts back in Wichita, had not been lying in his last pre-death delirium. Jubal felt a powerful elation rising in him. He must be close.

He felt his fingers gripping into claws, then fists, and imagined them around the throat of his wife's murderer.

Zack stumbled back, shaking, his hands raised to his mouth.

'Mister, you sure look mean!' he whispered.

'This Lee. Where is he now?'

'Dunno. God's truth, doc. I dunno. He rode in with the others—'

'Yes,' interrupted Kath's bitter voice. 'The murderers rode in and held us here, and the sheriff burned them out, and, and—' her voice broke.

'When was this?' Jubal's words lashed out like a stockwhip.

Kath laughed, almost dementedly, holding her fists balled before her. Her face betrayed a wild anger.

'Can't you guess how long ago? You a doctor!'

A little more of the story of this family and this decrepit farmhouse clicked into place.

But Jubal contented himself with a slow lift of his eyebrows and a drawled, 'Guess so.'

The Patterson family, stiff with poverty-stricken pride, wanted him to have nothing to do with their problems once he had successfully saved Beth. For his part, Jubal wanted none of their problems, either. He had enough of his own.

He felt pretty confident that the big hairy bear-like man sent

36

by Ben Agnew would soon discover he had slain Doc King and not Jubal Cade.

Then he would be back.

By that time Jubal intended to be on the trail of the scarfaced killer of his wife.

When he spoke after that drawling 'Guess so' his words shocked Kath and Zack, rocked them back. Jubal spoke with the forceful staccato of a rattler – or of a Gatling.

'Tell me all you know of scar-faced Lee. All of it. Now.'

They stuttered out their replies but there was little they could tell him. When the Crozley gang, led by one-eyed Zeke Croxley and his three sons, holed up at the Patterson place, Lee was with them. A shiftiness in the way Kath told him, a furtive manner so different from her usual directness made Jubal stare closely at her, trying to discover what secret she hid.

'Lee the father?' he said with sudden certain suspicion.

'No.' Kath clasped her hands, forcing herself to release the frantic tension that had held her. 'No. 'T'weren't him.'

'In that case,' Jubal told her. 'I'm not going to ask. I'm interested in Lee.'

Neither Kath nor Zack felt like asking this small but incredibly tough character just why he was interested in a two-gun outlaw.

The Croxley gang had held up a bank over in Larson City and had been trailed by lawmen through the territory and over the border and back again. They'd finally holed up at the Patterson place and there the sheriff of Rawson, Sheriff Gil Lovesay, had led a posse to burn them out. There had been a lot of shooting. Kath and Mat had been away at the time and the outlaws had found little opposition from the younger children. Jubal could guess what had happened, with Beth the only nubile girl about the place.

'They crippled Ma. She can't walk any more.' Kath's pallid features reflected the horror of that time, nine months ago.

'They escaped, 'cept for those the sheriff and the posse plugged. All the Croxleys, and Lee. And Smiling Leefe, too. He gave me a shiner that hurt real bad.' Zack rubbed his eye reflectively. 'The house was burning and they rode out

37

a-yelling and a-whooping and shooting real wild. Cain't say where they were headed.'

Jubal's excitement drained. Nine months was a long time. Long enough for the baby of a rape to come to full term. Long enough for the killer of his wife to be lost in the thousands of square miles of Plains country. He could have gone anywhere.

Yet a man left traces. The country was huge but it was sparsely populated. Stories travelled. He wouldn't have gone into the Indian Territory. South west lay the badlands. Texas might prove a haven. East – no, he wouldn't go east. Just as Ben Agnew could always find Jubal's trail, so Jubal made up his mind he would always find the trail of the scar-faced killer.

Anxious as he was to be gone, he reasoned that these kids might remember more details, given a little time. And his fatigue hit him anew, reminding him that the nap he'd had before Mat made his attempt on the baby had done little more than give him energy for the last scene. He surveyed the room, and the empty, untidy bunks, and he yawned.

'You still need that sleep, doctor,' advised Kath.

'Yes.'

'Take that bunk there – it's the softest.'

'Appreciate that.'

He put his grey derby down carefully.

'You think of anything else about Lee – you'll tell me?'

They both nodded without speaking.

Two tiny spots of colour glowed in Kath's pale cheeks. She regarded Jubal with a look that baffled him. A little breathlessly, she said: 'We do appreciate what you've done, Doctor Cade. Fixing up Beth and all. You do understand we had to kidnap you – make you come out here – don't you?'

'Sure,' said Jubal, rolling onto the bunk. 'It was a case of stand and deliver.'

CHAPTER FOUR

The sun had drifted past the meridian and threw sharp shadows towards the north east as Jubal guided his way along the rough trail towards Rawson. Around him stretched a mix of open rangeland and treed slopes, with a few scattered farmhouses here and there centring round patches of cultivation. The Patterson place had proved all he had expected, being decrepit and run down and needing the tireless application of constant work. For that a grown man was needed about the place, but the Patterson kids did as well as they could, and they survived. Just.

The trail wound down through broken bluffs, with the tree line lifting above. The area was well-watered, in contrast to the near-arid, treeless plains stretching away to the bar-line horizon. The bay jogged along and Jubal felt most of the aches and pains flowing away. He was not measurably nearer finding his wife's killer, merely following another scent that had gone stale and yet still lured him on. Kath and Zack and the others had added little to what they had already told him.

Perhaps the town gossips of Rawson would tell him more.

Halfway down the trail Jubal could tell by his horse's gait that something was wrong with the bay. With a grunt he hauled up and slid off. A check of the bay's hooves showed a stone wedged in the near hind hoof.

Jubal bent and caught the hoof, wedging the cannon up between his gripping knees. His knife flashed in the sun. With the same sure movements he would employ carrying out complicated surgery on a human patient, he carefully eased the stone out. It fell to the dirt with a harsh tinkle.

Jubal stood up and released the horse's leg. He patted the bay on the neck, soothing him.

'There, son, steady, steady. You're all fine now.'

The hoofbeats clattered down the trail above him and he

half-turned, looking up. His right hand remained on the bay's neck, but his left reached along the saddle towards the butt of the Spencer. The kids had given him back his rifle and revolver just before he pulled out, and Mat had stood with the Enfield centred on his back as he rode out.

The two riders coming carefully down the trail wore the checked shirts and denims of cowhands, with soft felt hats and scuffed ornate boots. They seemed in no hurry.

'Having some trouble, mister?'

'No trouble, thanks,' Jubal replied. 'Stone in his hoof.'

'Glad you caught it in time.'

They were both large-framed men, with the sun-burned plains look about them. They sat their horses long-stirruped, and the ponies were of that typical large chested, long fore-legged kind Jubal had found so strange after the European horses he had seen in England. There were lariats coiled at the saddles, but Jubal noted the way the men's holsters were tied down, thin black cords around their lower thighs. He did not move his hand away from his own saddle, but he tried to estimate his chances of reaching his shoulder rig before these gun-hands could draw. He knew he'd never make it.

Sweat began to ooze from Jubal's pores. He licked his lips, and felt the salt tackiness on his tongue.

'Been riding the trail long, mister?'

'Not long.'

'Seen you along o' the Patterson place, didn't we?'

The words were sharp through the drawl. The gunslingers sat their ponies, looking down on Jubal, their hands crossed casually on their pommels. The saddles were highfalutin, with a lot of fancy work, and hardly the kind cowhands would choose for the rough and tumble of working the herd.

'Maybe.'

'He says mebbe, Jed,' remarked the left hand gun.

'Now what kind of answer is that?' demanded Jed. His lower lip was very full, and pouted out, purple and shiny. 'Seems to me you either bin there or you ain't.'

'And if I said I had?'

'We-ell, I guess Mister Stoppard wouldn't take kindly to

that. No, sir, I'll allow he wouldn't take kindly to that at all. No, sir.'

'And who's Mister Stoppard?'

At this clear indication of Jubal's ignorance Jed looked across at his companion with a droll expression. He rolled his eyes. Then he lifted up in his stirrups and started to bring his right foot over.

'Can you beat that, Clay? Guy don't know who Mister Stoppard is.'

'Yet he goes avisiting the Pattersons. Seems he's one o' the Lord's abandoned, like the preacher says.'

At this, as Jed hit the ground and turned, alert, his right hand free and held waist level, Clay also swung out of the saddle.

Both men stood beside their horses, their feet and legs braced, their hands held in that old familiar way, fingers flexing. Jubal opened his mouth to speak and, instead, put his head down and leaped. He powered forward. Low down, he drove his bunched knuckles into Jed's groin and instantly, surging on, kicked Clay on the ankle. That was the nearest he could get.

Jed let out a shriek like a punctured steam boiler.

Clay yelled, more with anger than pain, and his hand darted down. It came up again with the Peacemaker snouting. Going on with his movement, Jubal pivoted and brought his knee up. He was inside the arc of Clay's fire.

Jubal's knee cap smashed sickeningly into Clay's groin.

The Colt exploded with a massive concussion, between the two men. The slug belted into the doubled-up Jed. It struck him just above his grasping hands, ripped into his belly. At the angle he was crouching the slug tore on diagonally downwards, exiting in an eruption of blood and bone from the shattered pelvis.

Jed fell to the ground, kicking spasmodically, shrieking with a shrill agony.

Clay let out a yell of pure horror.

'You bastard! You shot Jed—'

Jubal gave him no time. He turned hard into him, ramming his small but power-packed body in hard. The Colt snaked up.

41

Jubal got both his hands around Clay's wrist. Clay saw what he was trying to do and his face went taut. Sweat popped on his forehead.

For a brief space both men struggled to control the direction and aim of the gun.

Then Clay looped a haymaker. Jubal felt the soggy smash of the blow on his forehead. He grunted and drove in harder, bringing his knee up. Clay screeched and his locked muscles relaxed for the instant it required for Jubal to force the Colt all the way up.

The muzzle pressed against Clay's check shirt.

'No!' screamed Clay. 'No – we was only doing what Mister Stoppard—'

Then Jubal jammed in against the man's fist wrapped around the butt. The trigger came back, the hammer snicked and fell, and the Colt exploded lead into Clay's guts.

Quickly, Jubal released his grip and stepped back.

Clay let out a long moaning sigh, as the air was forced from his agonized lungs. Blood fountained from his mouth. For an instant he stood, foolishly, blood pouring from his mouth and nostrils, dribbling messily over his chin. His eyes were wide, not yet glazed. His arms hung loose, and the Colt, snagged around his trigger finger, still smoking.

Then he fell.

Not a spot of blood touched Jubal.

Stepping back Jubal got his breath. He was panting. His eyes snapped with that berserk fury he could barely control, the skin stretched taut over his high cheek-bones. Moving jerkily, he went across and picked up his derby. He wiped it carefully with a finger, then settled it on his black close-cropped hair.

'Two for the price of one,' he said, and spat.

He looked critically at the scene for a moment. Both men lay in their own blood, not yet dead but certain to die within a few minutes. Their groans tailed away as the silence of imminent death claimed them.

Moving with precision, Jubal bent over Jed, who had been shot by Clay. He lifted the gunhand's Colt and triggered a

42

quick shot into the sky, then he wrapped the dying man's hand around the gunbutt.

'Sleep easy, gunsel,' he said. 'You died with your trade in your hand.'

The ease with which he killed horrified Jubal Cade. But all the horror came after the deed. There had been no time to chop niceties when the gunslingers were clearly about to cut him down.

Past events had taught Jubal one certain rule – 'Shoot first and ask questions afterwards.'

He took off his derby and waved it at the dead men's horses.

'Go on. Git. Scat.'

Both horses carried a brand on their near-side haunches. A snake in the form of an S. S for Stoppard?

'G'wan, Git.'

The horses moved a little ways off, heads down, the reins dangling. Jubal paused, tense. Fresh hoofbeats sounded from down trail. Mingled clearly with the clip clop of hooves came the grating sound of wheels.

Jubal clapped his derby back on, grasped his horse's reins and then halted, staring down trail.

The red-wheeled gig he had seen in Seth's livery approached, drawn by a high-stepping gelding, black, well-groomed and with only a light scattering of dust marring its sleek coat.

But Jubal's eyes raked the form beneath the fringed canopy.

He saw a slight girlish figure, clad in clothes that were well-cut, tight at the bodice and flared at the hip and bust. The dress was pale grey and generously decorated with freshly-laundered lace. The shadows fell aslant her face. She flicked a whip and hauled back on the reins. The black gelding halted, blowing hard, almost spooked by the stink of fresh-spilled blood.

'What's happened?'

The girl's voice held no hint of fear or terror.

Jubal saw her hand, low in her lap, letting go the reins.

He spoke very quickly. He knew what a .41 Remington could do to a man's insides.

'Nothing to worry about, ma'am. These two are dead. I was

43

just riding down and heard the shots. They must have had an argument and it ended like this.'

For a long moment he wondered if she would believe him. All that mattered was that she wouldn't lift the little gun and drill him, on the off chance, just to make sure. Any girl who would drive a rig out alone knew how to take care of herself. He did not miss the Winchester stuck down its scabbard alongside the padded seat.

The shadow of the fringed canopy concealed the full details of her face, but as Jubal squinted up he saw her as a girl of undeniable beauty. The vividness of her mouth owed a deal to a pigment pot and her cheeks were darker than would normally be accepted, given that only girls of a certain kind used paint. Her hair was a bright corn colour, softened by the shadow, held by a bonnet of so fashionable a cut it must have been sold by a drummer straight off the boat from Paris. Her eyes surveyed Jubal, and the blocked trail, with the dead bodies sprawling in their last agonies.

Then :'Would you mind clearing the trail, mister? My horse is restless.'

Jubal laughed.

'Why, sure thing, ma'am. Anything to oblige a lady.'

'And you needn't get fresh with me.'

Now the derringer appeared openly, held in a small, lilac-gloved hand.

Jubal's smile grew strained. He doffed his derby.

'Name's Cade, ma'am – at your service.'

'The only service you can do me, Mister Cade, is to git them stiffs outta my way!'

Again Jubal's smile widened. He clapped his derby back on and obediently moved towards the limp corpse of Jed. He gripped the gunsel's shoulders and heaved him up against the weather-cut overhang, letting him slip down easy. He turned back for Clay and paused, looking at the girl in the gig.

'Kinda light rig for this country?'

Her tones sparkled back at him, and he knew at once she was almighty proud of her carriage – as she ought to be.

44

'This might not be a Brewster, but it was made in St Louis and is the best curricle in th' territory!'

'I'm sure.'

'Anyway, I don't often come this way – not any more.'

'Oh?'

She jerked the little Remington. By its glitter it was a fancy job, suitable for a woman's reticule. Jubal had once owned a similar gun, a plain model he'd won at poker from medical students in London. He bent to Clay and hoisted him up. Blood spouted. The girl's black gelding snorted and reared, hooves kicking wickedly.

The girl's startled scream was lost as the horse crashed back to earth. It lunged forward, almost knocking Jubal over.

'Hold him, you fool girl!' bellowed Jubal. He cast Clay aside and leaped for the horse. He missed. The beast's mouth clamped over the bit and it lunged on, kicking, rearing, its shoulder crashing into Jubal and knocking him spinning.

But at the last desperate minute he locked his fingers around a leather strap and fought to stay on his feet as he was dragged along. Luckily for him the runaway bolted uphill – had they been faced the other way and downhill Jubal would not have been so easily able to tame the horse.

He clung on, feeling the earth spinning around, half-seeing the rocky overhang and then the trail and then the gulf overlooking the plains. He clamped his hand on the back strap and tried to swing himself up for a grip on the bearing rein. His feet left the ground and then smashed back a jarring thud of pain.

His body was viciously whipped into the shaft, and he yelled as the polished wood struck into him. The girl was lashing away with her whip and screaming, which didn't help.

Jubal gave a tremendous leap as his feet fleetingly hit dirt and lifted himself, hauling with bunched muscles. He got a grip on the collar and made a last desperate lunge and secured the rein.

'Come round you bastard,' he yelled, and dragged the horse's head back by main force. He hauled the beast into the overhang, away from the sheer drop. The girl went on screaming.

Changing grips, he chanced letting go with one hand and gave the horse a belt. He hit the black real hard. He hit it again, and hauled, and felt the violent motion changing. If the light gig didn't fall to pieces from the battering – and if Jubal Cade didn't fall to pieces either – he'd have the rig under control soon. One red wheel hit a rock and flew into the air. Jubal gasped as something hard slogged into him.

With a final savage pull he dragged the horse's head around and braced his feet against the dirt trail. He skidded for some way, but finally he had the horse and gig under control. He stepped back, panting, his face red with exertion, and saw the horse was standing with flaring nostrils, blowing hard – but standing.

Quickly he stripped the bit back and settled the harness into place. Then he turned back to see how the girl fared.

She'd lost her gun.

Jubal walked back and stood looking at her under the hood. Now he could see her clearly.

She was a morsel. Painted, yes, dressed in so high a fashion she had to be what she was, yet she retained the essence of what Jubal recognized as womanhood. She held her hands to her bosom and swayed. Jubal got ready to catch her as she fell.

But: 'Thank you, Mister Cade. I owe you.'

He started to make the appropriate reply and she cut him off with a nasty bite to her words.

'If you hadn't thrown blood everywhere Blackie wouldn't have bolted! If there's any damage to my gig I'll make you pay, so help me!'

Her face showed she meant what she said. Abruptly, Jubal was tired of the farce. The stupid girl shouldn't be out alone. Her beauty would only further arouse trouble. And he felt the bangs and bashes of the wild horse-dragging added to his earlier aches and pains as an insult. All he wanted was a square meal, a bath, a shave and a bed. And he had no desire to share the bed with this girl. He glared up at her and fought the insane anger that consumed him.

Her body went rigid. She gripped the reins in a convulsive

46

hold that warned her horse that it had better not misbehave any more. Her face went white, and Jubal knew it was not delayed shock. Twin spots of red burned in her cheeks.

But she had spirit.

'Those two,' she said, nodding her head back. The bonnet had remained firmly pinned to her fair hair. 'I recognize them. Jed Holman and Clay Allnut – they was friends.' She regarded Jubal with a fresh bright inquisitive stare. 'Seen 'em lots of times in the McEnery House. Don't think they'd kill each other.'

'Can't say I've ever made their acquaintance,' said Jubal, easily, fighting down his anger at this stupid slip of a girl, anxious to be gone. 'But they sure killed each other.'

'They're Mister Stoppard's men. He won't be pleased.' And then she laughed. A high, shrill, almost desperate laugh. 'Not that there's much around here does please Mister Stoppard these days. And we all know why.'

'We do?'

'You're a stranger. Ain't none o' your business.'

'Reckon you're right,' allowed Jubal. 'And I aim to make it stay that way.'

'You got sense, mister.'

She flicked the reins. Jubal had cast a quick eye over the gig. The two-wheeled rig seemed in good shape. Although light, it was sturdily built. It had cost. Jubal didn't know who had paid for it, but he had a shrewd suspicion he knew how it had been earned.

The black gelding, now thoroughly chastened, moved forward quietly, set to haul on and behave itself.

Jubal stepped back.

He raised his derby. Even then, the gesture was not wholly ironic.

The gig rattled away up the trail. Jubal settled his derby back, bashed some of the loose dust from his clothes and started off back to his own horse.

He found the little .41 Remington over and under in the middle of the trail, halfway between the dead men and the point where he had brought the rig under control. He picked it

47

up. He'd no doubt see the girl again and could return it then.

He wondered if it was loaded, and checked. It wouldn't have surprised him to find an empty gun. But the derringer was loaded in both chambers. His smile was very wolfish as he went on down to his horse.

Turning to look back he saw the gig vanishing beyond the blunt ochre-coloured side of a bluff fringing the trail. He could feel the bruises where he'd been pounded, with the shaft bashing into his side and the horse tearing at his arms. He shook his head, the derringer in his hands.

'Well,' said Jubal Cade. 'That's one gig I won't want to play again too soon.'

CHAPTER FIVE

Sheriff Gil Lovesay hawked up a juicy gobbet of spit and smoked up a strike of dust from the street. He hitched his gun belt, pushed his hat over his eyes and swaggered up onto the boardwalk, headed for the law office. The sign creaked over the sagging door, but Jubal noted the iron bars at the single small window in front, and the toughness of the walls. They had been built early on from Prairie Marble, the sods cut over brick-size and packed in long even rows. Over the years the alignments had sagged. Inside, the sheriff's office had been faced with boarding and consisted of the usual outer office with an inner room and the cells leading off. A stove chuntered away to itself and the smell of heating coffee brought the saliva gushing into Jubal's mouth.

'Reckon they're dead enough,' commented the sheriff. He stalked through the swing gate, bashing it open casually with his thick thigh, and settled himself into the big bentwood chair, his belly sagging as his muscles relaxed.

Jubal, anxious to get to the hotel, nodded. The sheriff belched and spoke to his deputy.

'Ray, go git Harvey. Tell him he's got two more customers. Then you'd better ride out to Mister Stoppard. He'll fix the funeral with Harvey. He won't be pleased, I c'n tell you that.'

'You sure don't have to, sheriff. He was mighty partial to Jed and Clay.' Ray got up and slouched to the door. He was the sheriff's deputy, and wore his star over a sunken chest. He was tall and lanky with a prominent Adam's apple that bobbed when he spoke. But he carried his holster slung low like the sheriff's and there was no reason to suppose he could not handle the Colt.

Sheriff Lovesay flicked open a drawer in the big desk and came up with a chaw of tobacco. He bit off an end and got it started, meanwhile studying Jubal from beneath his craggy brows.

'Jis' found 'em on the trail, that right?'

Jubal nodded again. 'Like I said. I heard the gunshots, by the time I got there they were gone.'

'Yeah. Dead. Funny thing. They were friends. Can't see what'd make 'em shoot it out.'

'People do funny things, sheriff.'

'I'll make some enquiries. You'd better not leave town until I'm all through.'

Jubal's instinct to question the sheriff evaporated. Now would not be the best time. Even to himself, his own story sounded thin. He managed his smile, that turned his face into the semblance of a much younger man's, a trick that had served him well in the past.

'Then you can begin your enquiries with the young lady who witnessed what I witnessed.'

'Huh?' Sheriff Lovesay's chair crashed forward onto its two front legs. He stopped chewing.

'A young lady? Out on the trail by Medicine Bluffs? You'd better have a better explanation than that.'

Jubal described the girl and the rig. 'She came up same time as I did. Musta heard the shots.' He gestured with one hand out into the street where Deputy Ray way leading the two horses with their draped bundles over to the undertaker's. 'She drove off up the trail and I loaded these two and brought 'em in. Least I could do. She didn't give me her name.'

'That's Izah,' Lovesay told Jubal. 'Works in the McEnery House. Mister Dolman owns her.'

'Owns the McEnery House?'

'That as well.'

The sheriff turned his head and spat. A long juicy stream hit the spittoon dead centre and rang a brazen note into the hot afternoon stuffiness of the sheriff's office. He looked back at Jubal and grunted.

'What were you doing up there along Medicine Bluffs?'

'Just taking a ride. I find a constitutional does wonders for the liver. You should try it sometime, sheriff.'

Another grunt. 'I do enough riding without riding fer fun. It ain't natural.'

'Well, if I can't be of any more assistance to you, think I'll find me a meal and a bath.'

'Try the Star of Rawson, or the Jade Palace. They're not too expensive – they'll leave you yore pants to ride out in, Haw.'

Jubal looked down at his expensive and once elegant clothes. Of first-quality cloth, tailored in England, they were now in a sorry mess. He fingered a fresh rip in the grey pants, acquired in dragging a runaway horse under control.

'Appreciate that, sheriff.'

He went out without enlightening the sheriff that he fully intended to put up at the McEnery House. The place drew him for at least two reasons, quite apart from the meal and the bath.

As he unhitched his bay from the rail he saw Ray mounting up. The long deputy gave him a suspicious look.

'Give my regards to Mister Stoppard, Ray,' called Jubal. 'Tell him I'm sorry I didn't get there before his two hands shot themselves.'

Ray did not answer but swung up into the saddle. He loped down the main drag, leaning a little sideways in the saddle, his hat tipped back, clearly not looking forward to the ride out to Stoppard's Hissing S Ranch.

Harvey the undertaker, assisted by two older men, was just carrying the first of the corpses into the undertaker's parlour. Jubal shook his head and mounted up, turning towards the McEnery House. Pretty soon, when the sun dropped down below the horizon and the stars showed, Rawson would light up and the cowtown would burst into action. The heat held a somnolent quality. A few mangy dogs trailed their tails through the dust. A feed wagon rumbled past, the two big-boned horses leaning into their collars, the driver hunched and with his whip booted. A group of men stood arguing outside one of the saloons lining the main street. The telegraph operator stood before his open door, in the shade, his green eyeshade and apron marking his trade. Jubal marked it all as he jogged the bay gently towards the McEnery House.

Inside the hotel, with the long saloon opening off the

entrance hall and the stairway leading to the public rooms upstairs on the other side, there might have been problems had Jubal not slapped an Eagle onto the counter. The money softened up the expected opposition. Wichita had been kind to Jubal – apart from the red-haired man – but, even so, he was reaching the bottom of his stake.

They gave him Room Number Seven and promised to send up hot water and towels. Jubal intended to shave himself. He'd use the barber's as a means of information later. The stairs were polished. The floorboards held only a minimal number of splinters as he strode along the corridor, looking for Room Number Seven. From below the sounds of the street faded and died.

He dumped his valise, saddle-bags and the Spencer on the floor, shed his coat, loosened his tie, took off his boots, and lay on the bed. He felt dirty and sore and after a while he got up and started to bellow for the hot water. The oldster carrying water jug and basin and with a pile of towels almost spilled the lot.

'Hey, mister – easy!' he quavered.

Jubal stared at the basin.

'What's this?' he enquired in a nasty voice. 'I said I wanted a bath.'

'Bath house down the street,' announced the oldster. He blinked rheumy eyes. 'Fifty cents minimum. More with the fancy goods.'

Jubal fumed. But he was too weary to drag out again in the last of the heat. So he let the oldster, whose name was Sid, leave the water and towels. Then he set to work to wash the caked grey patina of dust and sweat from his superbly fit and muscular body. By the time he was through the water looked like a mud-creek after a storm, and the towels as though they'd been used to wipe out a barracks.

The room was pleasant enough, with a view of the street, but Jubal did not intend to spend much time there. The bed was reasonably comfortable, he wouldn't bother to unpack his gear and stow it in the big ponderous wardrobe. The washing facilities were adequate for a man who didn't need a bath, and the easy chair's one short leg gave it enough of a rock to sooth a man after a day's work.

Jubal placed his valise and the Spencer in the closet and carefully locked the door. He pocketed the key. Not that that would stop any halfway adept hotel clerk. But from what he had seen, the McEnery House appeared to be a high-class joint – certainly he could not afford to stay here long unless he re-couped some of his fortune.

And the Patterson family were unlikely to pay his fees.

He saw the cuff on the sleeve of his shirt and he frowned.

The cuff had already been turned, like the collar. He still had one decent shirt kept in reserve. Still frowning, he stripped off his dark grey coat and unbuttoned his vest. If he wanted to cut a figure in the McEnery House he would have to start right, the gold he'd flipped about would have only so much time in it.

He pulled the patched shirt over his head and threw it on the bed. His pants, too, could do with a brushing that would have to amount to a bashing with something hard to do any good. He sat down and hauled off his boots and wriggled the pants off. They were in a pitiful state. Soundlessly, Jubal pursed his lips together and regarded the state of his wardrobe. Travelling from New York, to St Louis, across the South West and points to hell beyond, had taken its toll. He was sitting with a clean shirt over his shoulders, without his pants, when the door to his room crashed open. A saloon girl, all scarlet silk and black bows and ribbons, with a fine expanse of bare shoulder and bosom, bounced in. Her powdered skin already shone with sweat. Her rouged and painted face snapped fiercely at him. Her black hair swirled.

'You the guy brought in Jed Holman?'

Modestly, Jubal reached over and put his derby on his lap.

'That's right.'

'Clay wouldn't kill him – and he Clay neither!' Her voice shrilled. 'Jed and me – we was planning – you musta kilt him! You murderer!'

She leaped for him, abandoned to passion, spittle flying from her painted mouth. Jubal rolled over on the bed out of her way, feeling all kinds of tarnation fool for being caught in this

53

situation. He tried to roll on over the edge of the bed and spring to his feet, but the girl threw a leg over him with a great rustling of voluminous petticoats. She clapped an arm across his throat. Her green eyes glittered into his deeply-set brown ones.

'You bastard! I'll kill you!'

He tried to speak and gagged. He thought his Adam's apple must be fair crushed.

With a jerk he broke her hold. He swivelled away.

'Now look here, miss. You've got it all wrong! Them two killed each other—'

'Liar!'

She reached for him again and his derby went spinning across the room as she raked out a red-taloned white hand.

Jubal figured this had gone far enough. He could get himself done a serious mischief like this.

He reached up and caught her arms above the elbows and started to force her back. Their faces were inches apart, glaring into the others's, one wild and savage with the lust to maim and kill, the other with the lively expectation of ending this brawl. Thus locked, Jubal became aware of another form in the doorway. He swivelled one eye, apprehensively.

The cowhand who stood there was dressed up in his best; fancy rowels, tight trousers of better material than the usual denim, a checked shirt that still showed the Chinese laundry creases. His neckerchief was bright red. Like his face. Jubal heard the click of the hammer on the Colt quite clearly as the would-be dude hauled back.

'Hey! Wait a spell!' called Jubal, and the girl, whose mingled smells of sweat and scent fair gagged him, screamed an oath and struggled to free her arms.

'You leggo o' Mary-Belle right smart, stranger. Gonna plug you where you lie.'

'I ain't lying!' yelled Jubal. 'She snuck up on me.'

'An' I snuck up on you. Start saying yore prayers.'

Now Jubal battled to hang on to the girl and drag her down onto him. He figured the cowhand wouldn't fire if the object of his fancy and, no doubt, his lust prevented a clean shot. All the time Jubal was wiggling his naked legs to the side of the bed,

54

aiming to swing off and duck down out of the line of fire.

'Let 'er go, you skunk!'

'You drop that Colt and maybe we can talk.'

'Ain't nuthin' to talk about. Yore plumb outta luck, fella. And keep still!'

Jubal got one leg over and then the other. If he was quick . . .

The girl shrieked obscene abuse at him, spitting in his face. He hung on to her arms and rolled. Totally unprepared for the drop she fell in a great rustling of skirts full on top of Jubal as he hit the bare floor.

All the breath was driven from his lungs. He felt her soft breasts squashing up against him and her scent gushed up into his face. He managed to drag some air into his tortured lungs and squirmed away when, with an almightly roar, the Colt went off. The bullet clanged into the bedpot. Jubal was in no mood for that kind of thing.

While the cowhand hauled back on the hammer Jubal released the girl and dived frantically for his legs. He made it – just. The girl raked out a hand and caught the flap at the back of his longjohns and held him. Jubal's chin hit the floor. He shook his head and through the din of starshells and skyrockets heard the ominous click of the hammer.

What a way to go!

Then a new voice, a deep, authoritative voice, said 'Just put that iron down nice and steady, Roach.' The click of a second hammer reinforced the words. 'Don't aim to have no shenanigans in my hotel.'

Jubal wriggled around on the floor and pushed up on his hands and knees. He peered up, feeling all kinds of tarnation fool all over again. The girl stared at his naked backside, and suddenly started to laugh. Roach spun his gun, releasing the hammer gently on the shell, slid it into his holster. The whole action was done with a slickness that told that this fellow, too, was no normal cowpoke but a hired gun.

'Don't aim to cause you no discomfort, Mister Dolman.'

'Nobody does, Roach, 'cept the folk who did up in Boot Hill.'

'This skunk was molesting Mary-Belle. Caught him redhanded.'

Mister Dolman peered past Roach at Jubal. Dolman wore a long-tailed black rancher-style coat over a fancy vest. His breeches were fawn and his boots of a polished silken brown. His face showed the paleness of a man who did not spend much time out in the searing sunshine. He affected a thin black moustache and his lips were red and moist.

The Galand and Somerville self-extractor in his hand pointed indifferently between Roach and Jubal. Pretty soon the revolver pointed only at Jubal. Jubal, on hands and knees, with Mary-Belle screaming in hysterics at his back, looked up. The blaze in his brown eyes, the way his skin tightened across his cheekbones, the flare of his nostrils and the thin bitter gash of his mouth made Dolman's face flinch in shock.

Then Jubal caught himself. He forced himself to rise.

He glared at Roach.

'You stupid idiot!' he said, shaking with fury. The sound of the slug belting past his ear and hitting the chamberpot still rang in his ears. 'You might have killed me!'

'Whut I was aimin' to do, mister.'

'Found Jed Holman and Clay Allnut out on the trail. They'd killed each other. This crazy girl seemes to think otherwise.'

At this Mary-Belle shrieked higher as her attack of hysterics mounted.

'Pardon me,' said Jubal.

He turned and struck the girl across the face. Not too hard – but not too softly, either. Enough to snap her out of it. She stopped laughing instantly and put a hand to her cheek. Her green eyes widened on Jubal.

The two men in the room sniggered.

Jubal whirled.

'What's so funny?'

'One thing's sure, stranger, you can't see it.'

'Told you. Mary-Belle made a mistake and was trying to convince me she was right. I was trying to convince her she was wrong.' He eyed the gunslinger, Roach. 'You want to make any more of it?'

Roach looked across at Mary-Belle and held out his hand.

'What you say, honey?'

'You – Roach. You don't own me – this little punk musta killed Jed and Clay! Don't see how – but he must have.'

'No!' snapped Jubal before the others could get to thinking overmuch on that one. 'Not true.' He looked levelly at Dolman. The hotel owner represented a breed of man whose position conferred favours and who took full advantage of that position. 'There was a witness. You ask her. Dolman, you ask Izah if I'm speaking the truth or not.'

The tension smoked between Dolman and Jubal.

'Izah?'

'Sure. She was there. She knows I couldn't have killed those two.'

Dolman's heavy florid face screwed up. The Galand and Somerville drooped as he raised his left hand and stroked across that bootstrap moustache.

'I'll ask Izah. Be sure of that.'

'You do that thing.'

Roach was now fully concerned for the girl. It was clear he had been hoping for her favours earlier and now that Jed Holman was dead he fancied his chances. 'You all right, honey? I'd'a killed the punk for you. Honest I would.' He reached out a hand again and took her arm, assisting her to the door. 'Can you bear to walk or shall I carry you?'

She turned and cast a meaningful look at Jubal.

Both men wore that puzzling sniggering expression.

Something on their minds was keeping Dolman and Roach happy. Yet Dolman, jerking the gun, said: 'I don't want any trouble in the McEnery House, you hear? You want to settle this, you settle it someplace else. For now, put it behind you, forget it, all of you.'

'Can you bear to do that, Mary-Belle?' demanded Roach, anxiously. 'Can you bear it? I'll make the punk—'

Mary-Belle laughed.

Jubal felt a draught.

He put a cautious hand down.

'Oh, surely,' Mary-Belle said, sniggering, still looking pointedly at Jubal. 'I c'n bear it and I c'n put it behind me. Guess I ain't the only one with a bare behind.'

CHAPTER SIX

In back of the Sundance Eating House slender shadows moved through the darkness. Jubal, just stepping down from the boardwalk to cross the street to the boardwalk fronting the Ace of Spades, whipped back into the cover of the weathered boards.

Anyone could be gunning for him now. He waited a moment or two, then eased down the alley between the Sundance and the Ace of Spades. He'd chosen to eat out of the McEnery House for obvious reasons. Now he wondered if that decision had been a wise one.

He heard the rattle of what sounded like a tin cup and then a quick hissing voice heshing up the offender. At that moment a great burst of laughter and yelling broke from the Ace of Spades. The batwing doors flew back. Two beefy men in aprons appeared carrying another man between them. They gave him the old one, two, three and then let fly.

He hit well out into the street, rolling over and over, fair spitting and cursing. His hat remained firmly wedged on his head all the time. He sat up and shook a fist and promised to deeprive them thar varmints o' there insides and backbones th' next time, yes, sirree.

Jubal made a face and eased down the alley.

A horse and rider clip-clopped past, and he froze.

When he reached the end he saw two dark forms bent over against the rear wall in back of the Sundance.

Coolly, Jubal studied the set-up. His Colt snugged in the shoulder rig under his coat. But something about those shadow forms . . .

Like a striking rattler Jubal powered forward. He got a firm grip around the frayed collars and said: 'If you try to kick or bite me or do anything silly I'll bash your fool heads together.'

Two gasps broke together.

'It's th' doc!'

'Doc Cade!'

He held them apart and twisted their heads up. They regarded him in the yellow light spilling from the Sundance's kitchen as though he'd popped through a trapdoor.

'Zack and Sam, Might've known.'

He saw the sack and guessed it held the leftovers scraped into the bins. He swallowed.

'How's Beth and the baby?'

They scuffed their bare toes in the dust.

'Well?'

'Beth's all right.'

'And the baby?'

He had decided he'd go back to the Patterson place before he left Rawson on the trail of the scar-faced murderer to make sure everything was still all right with Beth and the baby. A sudden alarm blossomed in him and he shook Zack.

'Well! Spit it out, son.'

'The baby's all right, I guess. Kath's looking after it.'

Jubal nodded, soberly. So Beth still hadn't brought herself to accept the child of a rape. Well, that was not so surprising.

A dark silhouette of a head and shoulders blocked the yellow light from the kitchen window. An irate voice bellowed.

'Git away from here, you varmints! I've got me a rifle on you an' I'll blast you iffen you don't git!'

Jubal released the boys' collars and they moved soundlessly into the shadows of the alley. A few more low-voiced queries brought answers that set a harsh vertical line between Jubal's eyebrows. He fished in his pants pocket.

'Here, Zack. Go git Beth some proper eats.'

The silver dollar flashed once in the starlight and then was snapped up in Zack's hand as a trout snaps a fly.

Jubal detailed what they should get.

Then he gave them each a friendly ruffle of their hair and sent them off. His last words were: 'Tell Kath I'll be along.'

One silver dollar was precious little between a family and starvation, but Jubal's poke was mighty thin right now. You

59

didn't run across too many slices of good fortune in life and Wichita, good as it was, wouldn't last for ever.

In Rawson, now, could he fare as well?

A woman screamed and Jubal heard the sound of running feet as he passed along the boardwalk before Hardman's store. The dry goods was shut and darkened. Then men scattered away from before the doors of the Rose of Tralee, brilliant light shafting out on to the dung-fouled dust of the street. The woman screamed again and a knot of men burst out past the crazily-swinging batswings. The knot separated into a group of onlookers and two men who faced each other, forty feet apart, crouched, panting, their hats pushed back.

Jubal sighed and edged along the boardwalk, aiming to get out of the line of fire, like every other sensible person in sight.

The two men began to stalk each other, crouched, heads jutting, their right hands drawn back, bent, hovering over gun-butts. Jubal could see the feral glitter in the eyes of the guy at the far end; the back of the one nearest him showed sweat stains on the hickory shirt, dark and somehow ominous, a portent of tragedy to come.

But Jubal's instincts were wrong.

The guy facing him went for his gun. The hickory-shirted man's hand snaked for his gunbutt, the thumb hauled back on the hammer as the muzzle cleared leather. The gun snouted up and belched smoke, held low, held firmly, held with a grip that sent the slug clean into the target's chest.

The men began a fierce argument among themselves. A woman dressed in saloon girl's clothes rushed shrieking into the street and threw herself on the fallen man. His fingers gripped and relaxed for a moment, letting the Colt drop into the dust. His body shuddered, the legs drawing up as blood stained across his chest. Then he let a deep guttural sigh escape. His body went rigid, then relaxed. His head lolled. The woman clasped him to herself, rocking back and forth, shrieking and yelling and moaning.

Jubal, seeing the man was dead and therefore past the help of doctoring, walked steadily on. There were people to deal with this kind of situation, and already Sheriff Lovesay was striding up the street, determined, right hand resting on the butt of his Colt, his jacket flapping.

'That wuz Steve Macandrew he done shot,' exclaimed a man nearest Jubal in the group. There was no way past them except by stepping off the boardwalk into the muck.

'Sure fast with a gun. Hey, Charlie – you ever seen a guy that fast before?'

'Kid Laurence, mebbe, over to Santa Fé.'

'Yeah,' considered the other, slowly, pondering. 'Mebbe.'

The man in the hickory shirt stood waiting quietly as Sheriff Lovesay stormed up. But there was little to be said. The deed had been done. Another shoot-out had ended in the death of a man. Mortician Harvey would be kept in business, that was sure.

Eventually, Jubal walked past. He gave the hickory shirted man a long veiled stare. Information was always valuable. And, with hope burning in him, he hungered for the sight of a four-inch scar furrowed across the killer's forehead, for the handsome, dissolute face of his wife's murderer to be revealed. But the lights from the Rose of Tralee showed him the square, bronzed, furrowed face of a man he had never encountered before. Grey hair showed under the low-crowned black felt hat. The man's denims were faded and patched, his boots plain and down-at-heel, as though he had done far too much walking about. He spoke softly with the sheriff and then walked away. He walked with a rolling gait, legs bent in the true cow-puncher's walk, but stiffly, as though his bones were seizing up through age.

'Jess Hawken,' he heard the men saying. 'Thought he was dead years ago.'

'Whut I heerd,' opined the barkeep, wiping his hands, going back into the saloon. 'Chantry Balderstone shot him, half a dozen years back, over to Tucson. Jess had taken to ridin' shotgun then, so they said.'

'It comes to 'em all, in time.'

'Yeah, but,' said Charlie, still excited, 'he sure is fast still.'

Jubal walked on. The names of notorious gunslingers were bandied about in hushed breaths all along the trails and in the

61

saloons of the West. A man gained a reputation and then other men sought to gain a brighter one by shooting him. It seemed to be a never-ending evil, gathering momentum as myths grew, springing up out of the ground and fed, as Jubal knew, by the lucrative magazine and book business back East.

Back in the McEnery House he stepped into the saloon and looked the place over. There was no sign of Izah among the brightly clad and painted girls laughing among the tables, working for their wages, making the customers happy. The long bar was jammed tight with drinkers, the bottles and glasses flashed in the kerosene lighting, for gas hadn't yet hit Rawson. The incessant clamour of men shouting and bragging and brawling, the clink of glass, the sudden bellow as a fight erupted only to be swiftly quenched by the bouncers – the whole gaudy, rowdy scene couldn't touch Jubal Cade. He just hoped he'd buffaloed Izah into supporting his story about what had happened back on the trail.

Carrying a single, small whiskey he went through the far doorway into the inner room where the gambling was of the more dedicated, professional kind. The faro wheel and the dice and all the other cheap tricks for relieving a cowpoke of his money didn't exist for Jubal – at the moment.

The lighting here was more discreet. The green baize table-tops allowed the pasteboards to flutter silently down onto the cloth. The men spoke in quieter tones. Jubal contented himself with standing beside the door – he was not fool enough to stand with his back to an opening – and looked over the set-up.

Slowly he drew a cheroot from his vest pocket and a match from his coat pocket. He struck the match on his boot and applied the flame and all the time his eyes did not leave the scene before him. He dragged in smoke, and exhaled, and flipped the match towards the brass ashtray by the archi-trave.

Those eyes of Jubal's, brown, deep-set, penetrating, shone steadily through the smoke of the cheroot, sizing up the men in the room.

Most were of the more prosperous sort in town. The dark-coloured frock-coats outnumbered the shirts and vests. There was even a black silk hat worn by the town banker. Jubal eyed him speculatively.

At his table sat four other men. One was a rancher, big and beefy, in a frock-coat thrown back to reveal the ornate pearl-handled revolver, belted rather high. His stake spread out before him and he wore the happy grin of a man winning and not giving a damn who knew. Another man with a check shirt, but whose vest bore ornate silver lacings, could be his top-kick, for they spoke together in tones that made that likely. The rancher was Clarence A. Manford, the foreman Luke Small.

The fourth man at the table wore a pearl-grey frock-coat, a grey low-crowned silk hat, and a silk vest of bright green, lavishly embroidered with gold thread. His face looked pale, paler than the banker's. His hands fluttered expertly as he dealt, the cards obeying him as though his dark, brooding eyes controlled them by forces unknown to normal men. For him, Jubal would spare a cartridge and scarcely miss its firing.

The last man intrigued Jubal. He was small, not much bigger than Jubal himself, with a round, cheerful face framed in iron-grey hair. His clothes were extraordinarily neat, well tailored, finely cut and well brushed. But his face showed a deep worry, and his hands trembled as he scooped up each card dealt. As the table was not playing stud, Jubal looked elsewhere, but he found his eyes dragged back as the little neat man burst out with an exclamation. His voice bore the unmistakable intonation of an Englishman.

'Confound it! My luck's right out tonight.'

'Play a few more hands, Mister Smith. Lady Luck will smile on you.' The rancher, Clarence A. Manford, smiled broadly as he spoke, raking in his winnings.

'Well, perhaps you are right, Mister Manford. A few more. And then, really, I must take my departure from you gentlemen. I am merely passing through from St Louis, you know—'

'Sure, sure,' said the grey-hatted man. His smile chilled Jubal, watching quietly through the smoke from his cheroot. 'You've a few dollars left.'

'Only a few, sir, to take me through to California.'

'Your ticket is paid for, sir,' said Manford. 'And your reputation is sound – at least, with me.'

Mister Smith looked down at his cards and then threw them away, pettishly. 'I wish the cards shared your belief in my reputation, sir. I declare I have never seen such bad luck before.'

Watching the play carefully, Jubal came to the conclusion that it was not bad luck that was ruining the Englishman. He could see from his position the quick and utterly effortless way the cardsharp manipulated the pasteboards. He could almost foretell the outcome of the next hand. Jubal might be an expert poker player, he might be able to spot a sharp better than most, but he was not prepared to go get himself killed because a mark was being plucked.

A waiter pushed through the door by Jubal, went silent-footed towards the table to bend down and whisper in the banker's ear.

The banker stood up, shuffling his stake together. 'Guess you'll have to excuse me, gents.' He pocketed his money and then spread his hands as though in explanation.

The rancher laughed.

'Yore plum loco for taking orders from that gel, Sam. Siddown and finish out the hand.'

'You know Martha.' The banker pushed his silk hat straight and started for the door. 'Ain't no use riling her none.'

The men's eyes watched as the banker left, and fastened on Jubal, standing quietly, the half-smoked cheroot slanted up in his teeth. The eyes were an invitation.

Jubal walked forward slowly.

He smiled and his face at once showed that innocent charm, accentuated by the two broken front teeth. He looked very young when he smiled.

'Be happy to sit in, gentlemen,' he said. He added in the customary form: 'Unless there's a house rule about not playing with strangers.'

The silence held. Then Manford spoke, heartily, rocking back in his chair, the big man of the moment.

'Sure, son. So long as yore money's good. Money ain't never strange.'

Jubal sat in the banker's vacated chair. He drew his whole wad out and plunked it down. The men eyed him, then the stake, then back to him. They nodded, as though satisfied.

The gambling man introduced himself as Dee Watson, from Kansas City way, he added, with a wave of his hand. A ring caught the lamplight and glinted frostily green.

Jubal nodded curtly, settling in the chair. Like the others, he kept his coat on. There were different ways of doing things in different schools in different towns.

He settled into the game easily, gently, dropping out as soon as he could if his hand held no promise, allowing himself to see the ante a couple of times, seldom raising. He watched every move. From the others' remarks he gathered they were half-sorry and half-not that the banker left. Apparently he enjoyed some reputation as a poker player.

This was not the kind of reputation they meant when they referred to Mister Smith, the Englishman. It transpired he was a tailor, making his way to California overland with a good stock and, having been bitten by the poker bug, was making his way across the continent with steadily diminishing supplies. At Rawson he'd been holed up for three weeks, hoping to win back some of what he had lost, and steadily dipping further and further into his stock of worsteds and high quality cloths on which he'd hoped to found his fortune in California.

'Like I says, Mister Smith, there's a trail o' well-dressed people all along the route back East!'

And Manford laughed until his face turned purple.

After his third kilter in a row, Jubal threw the cards down feeling he might as well call it a day. A hand with no pair and no card higher than a nine spelled a quick death in this company, for he summed them up as men who knew how to play and who could follow the lie of the cards. But he began to have grave doubts they could play in the same league as the gambling man, Dee Watson.

He won and lost a few dollars, gradually increasing his pile, getting lucky on drawing a pair to fill out a full house. Each

65

time he calculated the odds and played with the run of the game. At five-card draw there was little space for fancy work. Unless you faced a manipulator like Dee Watson ...

Dee Watson pushed back his chair and called for a drink and a cigar. He smiled on the company.

'Friends, this here game is a mite slow. Dragging. What do you say to raising the limit? Bring a sparkle to the eyes, give a little thump of blood to the heart – well, friends?'

Jubal was the last to nod assent.

'Ten dollars?'

'Make it fifty,' said Clarence A. Manford, the rancher, jovial with good humour, his winnings piled before him. Mister Smith looked thoughtful, but did not dissent.

The new game was agreed. A new deck of cards was brought and Watson broke the wrapper with an experienced flick of the fingers. The cards gleamed brightly in the lighting, slick and smooth.

The shuffle was long and careful, at the end Watson riffled the cards in a long diagonal line across the green beize. Then he flipped the end and all the cards toppled, one by one, to be scooped up and knocked swiftly into a neat deck. He shuffled with dexterous speed and planked the deck down in front of Jubal.

'Cut?'

Jubal cut.

He drew back in his chair and waited while the cards flipped out. He studied each one, making the necessary bid to Luke Small, the age, and eventually wound up with the ace of hearts, then the queen and jack of hearts, and the two of hearts and an odd spade. A bobtail. He let his gaze drift over Watson and fastened on the rancher. Manford could just about contain his excitement, but the way he squeezed his cards close to his chest told Jubal what he wanted to know.

The Englishman, Smith, also seemed about to burst out of his smart clothes.

The odds could be calculated exactly. That was one aspect to the art of poker. It was a one in five chance that Jubal could draw a card to fill the flush.

Looking back at his cards and then folding them flat together, he figured he wouldn't draw the king. That would be required elsewhere. Make it the eight, he figured, that would be about right. Maybe the seven if Watson had another play going.

Jubal drew the seven of hearts when he discarded his spade.

The tension around the table should not have existed. But the rancher, Manford, was too transparently jubilant with his luck for the night and the Englishman Smith showed the dawning of new hope. Only Manford's ramrod, Luke Small, folded with a soft-voiced 'Too rich for me, gents.'

The pot mounted as the fifty-dollar limit allowed the full raise each time. Jubal dropped his cards. He shook his head.

He offered no comment on his decision to fold.

Dee Watson favoured him with a sharp look. Jubal read a keen disappointment in the stare, as though Watson was shaken that a man should throw in a flush, ace high.

The betting went around and, as Jubal had known it would, the outcome sent Smith sagging in his chair, shattered. He held four kings.

Manford threw his cards down with a triumphant howl that changed to a disgusted throat-rattle. His straight flush in diamonds, eight high, looking so good, inducing him to pile his money into the pot, abruptly shrank as Dee Watson unveiled his straight flush in spades, queen high.

'Guess that's how Lady Luck shows her favours, boys.'

Watson's white hands raked in the bills. He allowed a small smile to disturb the thin moustache.

Smith was making small scratching motions with his fingers against the table-top. Luke Small shoved back, looking at his boss.

'All right if I mosey along to see the boys, Mister Manford? Guess they're getting kinda lit up around now.'

'Sure thing, Luke. Don't want Sheriff Lovesay getting his thick paws on 'em.'

Small's tough face went mean, then he nodded and went out. Dee Watson looked enquiringly around the table.

The next three hands went almost normally, as far as any

onlooker could judge. Smith won a hundred and perked up a trifle. Jubal leaned across, tilting his chair back, and called for a whiskey and another cigar. He tilted his head.

'Mister Smith. Watch Watson's left hand when he deals. Watch real hard.'

The waiter set up the drinks and for a moment the tension relaxed. Smith was shaking. He looked covertly at Jubal, and away. Jubal busied himself lighting his cheroot.

Dee Watson dealt. It was a beautiful thing to watch. Jubal knew the cards would have come around now into positions near enough for the sharp to have to make only minor adjustments. He made them. Manford took up his cards and by the way his hands gripped and then relaxed quickly, Jubal guessed Watson had decided the time was ripe to strike again. Smith held his hand down for a space, then lifted it and stared. A trickle of sweat ran down his face. He ignored it.

Jubal was dealt a busted straight, and he knew pretty well he'd fill it, outside straight and all. He sat back in his chair. The cheroot was not drawing well on account of Jubal had let the thing go out. Smith placed his ante and stayed and Jubal stayed and Manford allowed he'd stay, as well.

Jubal's next card did, indeed, fill the straight.

He sat back and casually put his hand into his pocket, sucking on his dead cheroot. Smith asked for two cards.

Manford looked across at Smith and a frown puckered his broad sunburned forehead below the hat.

Smith wet his lips. He nodded forward nervously. Watson dealt with that swift elbow jerking flick that sent the cards skimming over the table in the lamplight to settle like doves before Smith.

Smith staggered up. His face looked ghastly. Sweat damped the iron-grey hair. His lips were shaking.

'You cheated me, Watson! I saw! You didn't deal fair!'

Watson looked up and the evil glint in his eyes convinced Jubal that the man was a killer.

Jubal's hand closed around the butt of Izah's .41 Remington in his pocket. If she'd been in this evening to claim it, then Jubal's play would have been different.

Watson tipped back.

'Them's dangerous words, mister. You better take 'em back—'

'No! I will not take them back!' Smith stood, trembling with fury. He pointed an accusing finger. 'You've been cheating me, Watson! I want my money back!'

'No sucker takes his money back off Dee Watson.'

The gambler pushed back and the rapidity with which he whipped the derringer from his pocket showed he was fully conversant with the use of the little gun.

Smith choked back a cry. His hand flew to his mouth, plucking at his lips, whilst his outstretched hand trembled and spread as though to ward off the impact of the coming bullet.

The gun in the gambler's hand held rock steady. It was an ivory-stocked Williamson Derringer, probably one of a pair, single barrelled. It was the derringer among a plethora of copies that most resembled the original gun made by Henry Deringer. The rimfire .41 cartridge could send its slug to smash and kill Mister Smith without any trouble at all.

The gambler's face had paled. Sweat beaded his forehead.

He aimed the gun and his finger whitened on the trigger.

Jubal shot him dead centre of the forehead.

The Remington double-barrelled over and under Derringer barked out a harsh bellow of sound in the dimly-lit smoky room.

Watson swayed. His mouth hung open. The bullet smashed through the frontal bone of his skull, ploughed on through his brain, chewing up blood and grey matter as it went, driving the life out of Dee Watson, gambler.

For an instant he stood. The Williamson Derringer fell from his hand. It hit the table with a thud and Jubal did not flinch as it cracked off with a sharp bark of sound. The bullet slammed into a hanging lamp and brought it down in a blaze of splashing kerosene.

In seconds the McEnery House would be ablaze and then it would be gutted. Jubal stuffed Izah's little gun back into his pocket and leaped for the wall by the door. Blazing kerosene spread across the floor, eating at the carpet and the floorboards.

Smith yelled and staggered away. Manford leapt to his feet, yelling.

'Fire! Fire!'

The sand bucket placed by the door for just such emergencies weighed nothing as Jubal hefted it. He spun and powered towards the fallen lamp and the bright licking flames. He slewed the open mouth of the bucket across the fire, then back, spewing out a fountain of desert sand. The fires fizzled and sizzled at the edges of the sand built up at the centre.

'Git more sand!' bellowed Jubal. 'Jump!'

Waiters and saloon customers rushed in. More buckets were handed across. The smoke whipped away as the flames died. The sand built up.

Mister Dolman, cursing a blue streak, was there.

He saw Jubal.

'What in tarnation's going on?'

'Just a little altercation at cards, Dolman. But we didn't know Dee Watson was a pyromaniac.'

'What th' hell are you yammering about? Is that there fire out?'

'Yep. She's all through.'

'Through my carpet, you mean.'

'That as well.'

'Somebody's going to pay! Who started it! Look at the room—'

'He started it, Dolman,' said Clarence A. Manford. He pointed at the body of Dee Watson. 'It was his gun that brought the lamp down.'

'Yes, Mister Dolman. I can vouch for that.' Mister Smith looked a different man. Jubal had seen him hurling sand with the best of them . 'And if this gentleman had not shot, why, the bullet that brought down your lamp would have entered my heart.'

'That wouldn't have broken my heart none.'

Dolman swung on Jubal.

'Spoke to Izah. Seems you was telling the truth.'

'Gets to be a habit in time,' said Jubal.

'Don't make a habit of tangling with me.' Dolman strode to

70

the limp form of Watson, bent, and came up holding a fistful of money. That on the table lay untouched. 'Guess I'll take what's owed me from his roll.' He stared around, an arrogant, domineering man, high-coloured, intense. 'Any objection?'

'None,' said Jubal, quickly, 'Save we get what's ours, too. He was cheating. Slick, but stupid.'

The money was sorted out after Dolman shooed the folks out of the burned room and locked the door. The deal was made in his office, luxuriously furnished with goods hauled across the continent from New York, and to New York, from Paris and England. A man running a first-class saloon and hotel in Rawson could afford to pay for the best. Jubal sat in a deep leather chair and pulled on his cheroot and allowed he was due three hundred and fifty dollars from the dead man.

Manford's winnings had been eroded, but he remained ahead.

As Jubal told Smith when they were standing at the bar outside the office, conscious of the rolls in their pockets: 'Dee Watson was fattening up Manford for the kill. As soon as the banker left he had a clear enough hand. You were the pigeon, Mister Smith, the act to take the light off Watson.'

'You got my money back, Mr Cade. I'm most grateful. If there was some way I could repay you – saving my life as well.'

Jubal downed what he promised himself would be the last whiskey of the night. He wiped his mouth and started to speak, and saw the light in Smith's eyes.

'I've got it, Mr Cade! Capital, capital. By Jove, that's it!'

'It is?'

'Of course. I'm the best tailor this side of St Louis – and judging by the cut of these people's clothes, the best bespoke tailor in the whole of America. And, Mr Cade, I see by your clothes you are a man of taste.'

'Pretty tasteless now,' Jubal replied, shaking his head. He told Smith the story of his clothes and Smith nodded his appreciation:

'A most highly regarded house, my dear Mr Cade. Their cutting is an art. I have a few private doubts as to their trimming and—' He stopped and smiled. 'Forgive me. I feel so cut off out here in the desert—'

'Folks in Rawson wouldn't like you to call their city the desert, Mr Smith.'

'No? Oh, dear. I don't mean to offend.'

Then his idea took possession of Smith again and he looked most attentively at Jubal.

'Yes. You are deceptive, Mr Cade. There is more to you than meets the eye. And I shall do my very best work. I'll make you a suit that will be the envy of anyone in London. Believe me, my dear sir, it will be a pleasure.'

At Jubal's quick frown he stepped back, puzzled.

'You are not offended, Mr Cade?'

'No, Mr Smith. It suits me fine.'

CHAPTER SEVEN

Sweat was pouring down his agonized face, his closed eyelids were bunched into two tight mounds, his lips were drawn, the choked scream echoing through clenched teeth. Up there on the crazy balcony the red-eyed, parchment-skinned, snowy-haired albino, Saul Klein, appeared wolfishly triumphant, the twin Russians in his hands belching flame and smoke. Bullets tore and crashed about Jubal as the blind boy, Andy, headed into the deserted saloon carrying the Spencer, acting as though he could see where he was going.

Backwards and forwards on the soaked pillow the desperate, sweat-sheened head of Jubal thrashed. He moaned and fought the bedclothes. Now he had the Spencer in his hands, was feverishly levering the action, ignoring the lashing pain in his side where one of Klein's bullets had ploughed into him, the blood oozing from the wound in a crimson stream.

The hammer of the Spencer cracked forward and the rifle spat .30 calibre lead at the albino on the balcony. Pain suddenly clawed at Jubal's arm, but he ignored it and slammed the Spencer's lever again.

So he shot Klein. He sent bullets punching into the albino, saw the abruptly shocked expression seize the man's pallid features, his mouth opening in the first shriek of pain, saw a bullet plough through the distended mouth and smash out of the neck spraying blood. The albino pitched into the rotted wood of the balcony, crashed through and fell to the floor in a red-tinged cloud of dust.

Jubal moaned to himself, his hands gripping into fists, his legs kicking the bedclothes there in a room in the McEnery House in Rawson. So he had shot Klein. And he had turned to find Andy, the blind boy on whom he had lavished so much love and affection, for whom he had suffered so much pain and blood—

The dream didn't go on much beyond that point.

The agony, the stark brutality of it, usually awoke Jubal as he staggered across the smoke-filled room of the saloon to where Andy had pitched forward onto his face on the dirty floor, the blood pumping out of that obscene hole in his back.

The scream trailed away like the desolate howl of a lobo wolf.

Jubal crashed from the bed, entangled in the sweat-fouled bedclothes.

He woke up, knowing the dream had struck again, and so lay on the floor for a space, panting, filled with misery, sick with an insane despair that threatened to overwhelm him.

There wasn't much he remembered after that.

He thought there'd been a grave and a marker, and a few broken words. The names of towns ghosted up, in no special order, crazy places were there had been fights and brawls, wild drinking, killings. Yes, there had been killings.

Dodge City? Yes, and Denver. Santa Fé? He just didn't give a damn. He'd been on a wild swing around the country, and had really only become his own man again at Wichita. There he'd found the red-haired man who had subsequently died with a Bowie in his guts and news of Lee Kincaid, the scar-faced killer, on his lips.

It had seemed to Jubal that Ben Agnew, who had sent the albino on a kidnap mission, would continue to seek him out. Ben Agnew would pay for the death of Andy Prescott.

That was written, too.

Suddenly the door slammed back and lamplight splashed across the room, highlighting Jubal sweatily entangled among the bedclothes.

'What in tarnation's goin' on here?'

In the open doorway stood the tall form of Jess Hawken. He wore a long nightshirt. In his left hand the lamp shed its golden rays upon the scene. In his right hand he gripped a Colt Army model 1860, the cylinder bored through to take the .44 Henry rimfire cartridge. The muzzle did not waver.

Then, in a sharper tone as Hawken took in the scene: 'You

all right, mister? Yo' plumb shook the hotel down to its breeches.'

'All right,' Jubal said, struggling up. 'Bad dream.'

'Bad dream? Don't believe in 'em meself.'

Then he laughed, showing yellowed teeth with a goodly proportion missing. 'Kilt too many hombres to start a-worritin' about 'em now.'

'Yes, I saw. Real handy with a gun.'

'Usta be. Gittin' old. Rheumatics gitting to my bones.' Hawken eyed Jubal coldly. 'Fergit I said that, son.'

'Forgotten,' Jubal assured him soberly.

Hawken licked his lips.

'Ain't got a spot of the real stuff handy, have you, son?'

' 'Fraid not.'

Again Hawken licked his lips. His deep-set eyes held a look of profound calculation. 'You sure you're all right?'

Jubal sat back on the bed and hauled the clothes up any old how.

'Sure. I'll say good night, then. Thanks for looking in.'

'You sure you ain't got a bottle around?'

'I'm sure.' Suddenly Jubal realized he could stand a stiff whiskey, and damn his resolutions. Every time he suffered that particular nightmare, he felt washed out, drained, exhausted.

'Why don't we go downstairs and see what we can find?'

'Good idea, son. I don't mind if I do.'

As Jubal rose he guessed already who would be paying.

Jubal hauled on his pants and slid his vest over his shirt. Then he strapped on the shoulder rig. Hawken looked on, vastly amused.

'You'd never last with that rig, son, out there where it's tough.'

Jubal blinked. Hawken's right hand was empty.

Moving with the speed of a striking panther, Hawken drove his empty hand into a slit in the side of his nightshirt. The hand came out gripped into a fist, the Army Colt snouting up, the hammer already back. With a grim laugh, Hawken let the hammer down gently, spun the gun and flicked it back into the

75

holster on a low-hung belt around his waist under the night-shirt.

'Feel nekkid without,' he said, casually.

Jubal guessed the performance was intended to do double duty this time of night. He followed the gunslinger out of the room, carefully locking the door and putting the key in his vest pocket. His mouth was as dry as the Gila Desert.

The place was deserted below, with the chairs upturned, the floor empty, and a single lamp burning over the end of the long bar. Here Hawken reached up a long arm and hauled down a bottle of redeye.

He poured two shot glasses and then eyed Jubal over the brim of the one he raised before his mouth.

'I'll give you a toast,' he said, his mouth making thirsty puckering motions.

'Sure.'

'Here's to a greased gun and a lead coffin.'

Deciding there was little to say to that, Jubal drank. The fierce stuff hit him in the pit of the stomach. He gasped and wiped his lips.

' 'Nother?'

'One.'

'Me, too.'

Jess Hawken downed the second drink at record speed and immediately poured another. He regarded it with great satisfaction.

'Thought you said only one?'

'Sure I did, son. One at a time. Always moderate in my drinking. One drink at a time. Cain't git into trouble thata-ways.'

'That makes sense.'

They fell into the lazy, disjointed conversation of men aroused after midnight. Hawken vouchsafed no reasons why he was in Rawson and neither did Jubal. The talk centred around general topics, the town, the people, and Jubal got a quick flash of anger from the gunslinger as the name of Stoppard was mentioned.

'Knew his paw, back in th' old days. Went buffalo-skinning

76

with him, up around Clear Springs, and over to the Platte.' He drank reflectively. 'Them was the days before they kilt the buffaloes for fun, or to git at the Injuns.'

He shook his head, remembering a time of pain. 'Guess old Jim stuck by the Grey, right through. Didn't do him nary no harm around here, in course.'

Jubal was courteous enough not to press for any details. Which side a man had fought on, the Blue or the Grey, remained between him and God as far as Jubal was concerned.

'So it's his son that has the town buffaloed?'

'Tarnation right it is. None o' my business. But that skunk Abe Stoppard has his fist around the neck of near everyone in Rawson. He runs 'em all. Th' bank, Sheriff Lovesay, Dolman, the Cattlemen's Association — leastways, not all o' them, to be sure.'

Jubal remembered the flash of anger in Clarence A. Manford's ramrod's face at the mention of Sheriff Lovesay.

A wan wash of blue moonlight filtered through the windows and the lamp's yellow glow seemed to shrink in the shadowy space of the bar. The abandoned chairs and tables, the still fargo wheel, the bottle display, the gilt-framed pictures of rubicund naked women adorning the walls, the tiny stage with the red velvet curtains, the upright piano off to the side, all appeared to grow blue-rimmed presences, as though glowering down on the two men invading their nocturnal privacy. Hawken downed another drink and poured again immediately. Jubal made no attempt to keep up with him.

The story came out, slowly, disjointed, fragment by fragment. And, with it, the reason for Jess Hawken's return to Rawson, a return that appeared to be a visit from the grave.

'Purty little thing, she was. Annie Stoppard. Always pleasant to me, laughing and friendly, but she never once thought of me anyways else than as a no-good panhandler. And me — allus treated her like one o' the boys. Couldn't kinda rouse up the nerve to tell her any different.'

Jubal listened. Old man Stoppard had been considerably older than Jess Hawken, and his daughter Annie, although younger than Hawken, should by rights have married her

77

father's young friend and partner. But it hadn't worked out like that.

'Back in '55 young Mat got her. Wore th' Blue then, wore th' Grey after. Fine upstanding feller, clean, good shot, damnedest man on a horse you've seen. Turned Annie's head. I cleared out, drifted around, saw th' country. Berdan's Sharpshooters – seen it all.'

He drank again. An alcoholic melancholy gripped him. Jubal listened. Annie Stoppard's gallant cavalry husband had died. But old man Stoppard had remained good to her, even though she had not married as he would have wished, and here Jubal caught Hawken's honest appraisal of the situation. It wasn't a rousing gunslinger like Hawken that Stoppard would have wished his daughter to marry. His son, Abe Stoppard, had married – 'Dangdest thin-lipped woman you ever want to steer clear of,' as Hawken put it. When old man Stoppard died and Abe inherited the Hissing S spread, his wife had forced him to throw Annie and her children out. They were given a patch of land on the edge of the spread and left to fend for themselves.

Jubal lifted his glass and turned it in the lamp's glow.

'You didn't mention Annie's husband's name. Would it be Patterson?'

'Sure? Didn't I say?'

'You seen Mrs Patterson – since you came back to Rawson?'

Hawken tossed the drink back and poured and drank another before he shook his head sourly. 'Nope.'

Jubal did not pry.

Hawken pushed an unsteady hand through his grey hair.

'Don't want to rile her up none. I'm no good fer her.'

'She'd be pleased to see you.' Then Jubal told him of his own experiences out at the Patterson place. Hawken listened in total silence. When Jubal had finished, Hawken put a full glass onto the counter and stared blankly at it for some time.

Then: 'The Croxley Boys?'

'You know 'em?'

Jubal tensed. Jess Hawken was a wild gunslinger of the frontier towns – well, he had been, even if he claimed he was old and slow and rheumaticky now – and it was a good chance he

78

would know the Croxley gang and, with them, the scar-faced killer.

'Nope.'

Jubal sagged. He fought the disappointment. He had faced disappointment before.

He gave a description of Lee Kincaid.

'Nope. Never set eyes on him.'

He gave a description of the big hairy bear-like man who had been sent, he believed, by Ben Agnew to kill him and who had mistakenly killed Doc King.

'Yeah. That sure sounds like Arnie Javaro. Real mean bastard, despite being so big and hairy. Thinks he's good with a gun.'

'Is he?'

'Yeah,' Hawken allowed, and looked again at his untouched glass.

'Local?'

'Hell, no. Like me. Goes where there's a job, or the pickings look good.' Hawken sighed, and, at last, picked up the glass. 'I'm through, Cade. All through. I've come back to Rawson to stake me a claim up in Boot Hill. Maybe fix Harvey to put me up a fancy marker. But Javaro – he's still a-running and a-shooting and a-killin'.'

'You weren't all through this afternoon. That was a fancy piece of shooting—'

The big gunslinger grimaced. 'You get 'em all over. No matter where you go. Gun punks, think they'll git a big reputation if they plug ole Jess Hawken. I warned him, real nice, but the dame egged him on. Stupid bitch. I tried to hit him in th' shoulder, but I'm old and slow, too far gone for fancy shooting.'

'Then,' said Jubal softly. 'I reckon that makes you more deadly than ever.'

'It does? Yeah, I guess you're right. It does.'

Jubal laughed softly, and reached for what he intended to be his last drink, and realized the bottle was empty. Hawken barely showed any effects. Hard liquor he could take, a surcease to the agonies in him, a dulling of the pain of merciless time.

'None o' my business, of course, Mr Hawken. But I'd take it as a favour if you'd go out and see Mrs Patterson.'

Hawken stared wearily at Jubal.

'I thank you for whut yo' done for young Beth. Seems Annie – well, mebbe I'll take a swing out around there.'

The blue-tinged moon shadows in the long bar held an eerie look. The lamp threw its oval of gold across the counter and the floor. Jubal took out a coin and tossed it on to the polished bartop. It winked in the light, ringing, spinning.

'Think I'll hit the hay.'

The thud of a heavy door punctuated his words. The sound of a hard voice, yelling in anger, and then a woman's scream resounded down the stairs. Quick footfalls across the corridor above and the slamming of the door. A woman sobbing. Hawken looked up, his furrowed, bronzed face set.

'Somebody don't like Dolman's wares,' he opined.

A shadow appeared at the head of the stairs. Both men looked up, their hands held close to their gun butts.

Slowly, one step at a time, a woman descended the curving stairs from the balcony overlooking the long, shadow-haunted saloon. She wore a nightdress of expensive lace, ripped across a shoulder; without a peignoir or pelisse, the lace hanging carelessly off her body. She held her arms limply at her sides, making no attempt to cover up her nakedness, and one firm breast showed through the lace ruffles, round and plump, pink-tipped and mysterious in the half light.

Her face ran with tears. Thick, ugly bruises showed on her cheeks. One eye was already puffed. Her mouth hung lopsidedly. Jubal noticed her naked feet as she descended the stairs. Each foot showed in turn under the lace hem of the nightdress, like shy animals peeping out from cover.

'Izah!' he said, taking a step forward, his hand dropping away from his shoulder rig.

She saw him and stopped, one hand going to the banister as she swayed.

She stared.

At his side, Jess Hawken made no sound or move.

'You all right, Izah?' A stupid question.

Then she laughed. A harsh cackling sob that broke up from deep within her and welled out into the shadowy room.

She tottered forward. Her hand slipped on the banister.

She fell forward helplessly.

Jubal hurled himself at the stairway, leaping up five steps. He caught the girl around the shoulders and tried to hold her up. Her legs hit the treads, making heavy, thumping sounds. All the time she wailed in that stomach-shrivelling screech that drove sharp nails through a man's temples.

Hawken stepped forward as Jubal gently lowered the girl to the floor. The big gunslinger stared down, his face unreadable in shadow.

'Izah?' He spoke hesitantly.

The girl looked up into Jubal's face and stopped her wild sobbing. She swallowed down, gulping convulsively. Her face was a mess.

'Mister Cade – see what you done?'

'Me?' Jubal eased her down. He stood up, turning to Hawken. 'Keep an eye on her, please, Mr Hawken. I just got to get my bag.'

"Uh?' Hawken swung his head up, away from Izah, to stare in puzzlement at Jubal.

Jubal puffed a sigh. 'Guess the whole town knows by now. I'm a doctor. I don't spread it around.'

'You could have fooled me.'

'I aim to.'

Izah screamed.

'You bastard, Cade – *Doctor* Cade, is it! You rotten skunk! See what you gone done to me?'

'Won't be a minute,' Jubal said, starting to run up the stairs.

'I'll be here, doc,' called Hawken.

Jubal paused. He turned, one hand on the banister. He looked down on the old gunhand.

'Mister Hawken – make it Jubal if you must, not doc.'

'That sets fine by me – iffen you make it Jess.'

Jubal nodded and ran on up the stairs.

Izah stared up through her one good eye.

'Jess Hawken?'

'Jist rest easy, Izah. Jubal'll see to you, like he says. Then we'll find out who done this to yuh and return the compliment. Now, lie easy. Your ma would be in a fine fret if she could see you now.'

At this Izah's wild, near-hysterical sobs broke out again. Hawken looked down helplessly, his grizzled head shaking from side to side as he tried to hush up the distraught girl.

Jubal returned with his valise and started to work on Izah's face at once. He pulled the lace nightdress across her exposed breast with a matter-of-fact flick that concealed the quick response to beauty that had not yet been killed in him. He washed the blood away carefully, using a little whiskey and water, and applied salve. The worst damage had come from what must have been a heavy signet ring. It had cut the skin in three places on her soft cheeks. Jubal swore as he applied himself to mending the damage. Izah moaned softly.

'We'll carry you back to your room, Izah,' he said, standing up, stretching, and then reaching over to click his valise shut with what he hoped was a gesture of finality.

She laughed.

The laugh was more of a continuation of her wild sobbing; she could not control the spasms that shook her.

Jubal shook his head.

'Had to slap one hysterical girl tonight, Izah. Mary-Belle. Can't slap you around the face now I've fixed you up. If you don't quit that squawking I'll have to slap you someplace else.'

She gulped, choking back her pain and presently broke into a low-keyed sniffling.

Hawken said in a grim, grating voice: 'Afore we takes you back to your room, Izah, we wanta know who did this to you? What skunk'd lay a hand on a fine girl like you?'

She stared up at him, the tears now coursing freely, her face pinched under the salve and the dressings.

'Won't do no good.' Her voice was a shadow among shadows. 'Threw me out. No room to go to.'

'Tell me,' insisted Hawken. 'Ain't finished this yet.'

'He'll kill you as soon as look at you.'

'Mebbe. Who?'

Izah let a moan break through her bruised lips.

Thoughtfully, Jubal said: 'You know Izah, Jess?'

'Did. Long time ago. But she sure has growed. Looks plumb like her mother.'

Jubal nodded.

He licked his lips. What he was going to say now held danger, but he did not think Izah would speak and, although strictly speaking it was none of his business, he fancied a real purpose in life would give the has-been gunslinger a fresh lease on his life. Even revenge, which is not sweet but carries dust and ashes, can serve a purpose, as Jubal knew only too well though he would not admit it.

'Don't get me wrong, Jess,' he said, speaking carefully. 'Heard around town folk saying as Dolman would be the man—' Then, chancing it all, he added, 'They said Dolman owned Izah.'

Hawken's jaw muscles jumped. His eyes in the lamplight gleamed like those of a mountain lion, and then went hooded and dead. His hands moved – just the once, just the single quick instinctive clawing motion – then he was still.

'Dolman. Guess I'll pay him a little visit.'

'Not tonight, Jess.' Jubal spoke quickly. 'Daylight. With witnesses.'

'Huh?'

Izah levered up. Her face showed anger. She fairly spat at Jubal.

'You sure have a big mouth, doc. First you tell Dolman where you saw me. Then you tell on Dolman – you don't know it was Dolman did this to me.'

'Suppose you tell me who did?'

She sank back, shuddering.

Jubal went on: 'And what's wrong in getting you to back my story? The Sheriff will want to speak to you – Jed and Clay killed themselves, and you can prove it.'

Izah moaned.

Hawken bent over the girl and then half-turned to glare up at Jubal.

'Easy, doc – Jubal.'

In his attitude showed the savage care of a parent for young. But Jubal guessed Jess Hawken was not this girl's father. He wondered – although it was no concern of his – how she had explained away her parentage to Dolman, who was in Stoppard's pocket. Probably she had not done so. Probably she had swung back to Rawson with another name. That was the likely explanation and fitted the known facts.

But then – he bent again, putting his valise down.

'You telling me Dolman didn't do this, Izah?'

She rolled her head. Hawken supported her and his hard eyes with the chiselled crow's-feet at the corners regarded Jubal with a new light.

'What you say is right, Jubal,' he cut in. 'Leave it to th' morning. Then Izah'll feel better. She c'n stay in my room tonight.'

Jubal nodded. 'And you?'

'Guess I'll find me another bottle and watch the sun up down here.'

The old gunslinger evidently meant it when he said he'd come back to Rawson to live out the rest of his life. He was sage enough to see the truth in Jubal's argument. With a gunfight and a death in the middle of the night, no one would want Hawken around Rawson. In broad daylight, with witnesses, it would be another scene entirely.

They settled it at that, although Jubal was not entirely satisfied, and saw Izah into Hawken's room. Hawken took himself off to the bar again and Jubal accompanied him for a last nightcap.

'In the morning, then, Jess.'

'Surely.' The gunfighter tossed the first of the bottle back. So, feeling the weight of oppression on him, Jubal went back up the stairs joylessly to bed.

CHAPTER EIGHT

The first thing Jubal Cade did when he opened his eyes next morning was to reach for the Spencer propped against the bed-head. The feel of the old gun in his hands reminded him of the ever-present need for weapons along the frontier. The Spencer had been converted from a carbine to a .30 calibre rifle and the gun was getting long in the tooth now. But she still levered with a smooth precision and she shot straight.

He spent a little time on the rifle, cleaning and oiling, before he gave a thought to himself.

With hot water and towels brought by Sid he washed and shaved and gave a perfunctory brush to his clothes. Then he went down to find out about breakfast.

Wiping his lips after bacon, eggs and pancakes, and with the taste of the bitter coffee still in his mouth, he headed out of the dining-room. Mister Smith caught him up, smiling, looking resplendent in his English clothes.

'Doctor Cade, I believe! Good morning to you, sir. You have not forgotten our arrangement I trust.'

''Morning, Mr Smith. No, sir, I have not.'

'Then if you will kindly step into my room I shall be pleased to begin.'

Smiling, Jubal followed, and was carefully measured. Smith whistled as he stepped back and draped his tape around his neck.

'You are, as I have said, Doctor Cade, a remarkable man. Like me, you are small of stature. Yet your chest will demand expert cutting—'

'That's what the man in London said.'

Smith bobbed his head. 'And I believe here in this barbaric land a small pocket or two, in inconspicuous places, would not come amiss?'

'Right,' said Jubal, laconically, smiling so that his two broken front teeth gave him that deceptive air of innocent youth. 'But I lost my derringer a ways back. And I forgot to return the lady's last night.'

'I beg your pardon?'

'Nothing, Mr Smith. Now, if you'll forgive me, I have a matter that won't wait.'

Looking in on Jess Hawken's room, Jubal gained no answer to his knock. He knocked again and called softly. No reply.

Eventually he pushed the door open.

The room was empty. The bed clothes lay tangled on the floor. All the drawers and closet doors stood wide, as though ripped open in a frenzy and left. The room showed no sign of occupation. A frown creasing his forehead, Jubal took a look around and then left.

Jess Hawken had clearly taken upon himself the chore of looking after Izah – whose real name, no matter what name she might be using now, was Izah Patterson – and from his family connections, that was probably a good thing. Jubal had no intention to get mixed up in a family feud and he reflected that his sole concern was the welfare of Beth and the baby. They were, however oddly they had come into his care, his patients and to them he owed his duty.

There was no sign of Dolman as Jubal walked down the public staircase of the McEnery House and through the lobby. Sid gave him a leer from his booth and a couple of men pushed through in a hurry to get out on to the street. The place was hushed with that dead hotel feeling. Later on the usual rowdiness would erupt and the noise and whooping-it-up would go on again to the small hours. Jubal stepped through onto the porch and started down the street heading for the law office.

The sound of galloping hoofbeats thundered up from the far end of the street.

Jubal moved back into the shadow of the porch fronting a gunshop as other people scuttled off the street to safety. When cowpokes came raging through, no matter what time of day, sensible people made themselves scarce.

The gunsmith came to his door. He shoved a pair of wire-framed spectacles higher on his nose and wiped oily hands on a rag. He peered up the street and made a tching sound. He saw Jubal standing quietly.

'The Hissing S boys,' he said. 'Kinda early, though.'

He looked more closely at Jubal, at the torn and scuffed clothes that were clearly not those of a cowpoke. At the grey derby. He squinted through the spectacles.

'You're Doc Cade, that right, doc?'

'Something the matter with you?'

'Matter? Naw, son. I'm fitter'n I've ever bin. Comes o' not drinking cheap whiskey and staying away from the cathouse.'

'Then I'm Cade.'

The galloping horses slowed before the McEnery House. There were a dozen punchers, dressed in denims and checked shirts, with decorated vests, Stetsons jammed on shaggy heads. A man in a rancher's frock-coat and flared breeches hauled up. He sat solidly on his horse, a white stallion with a long silky mane. His saddle and rig were thick with silver bullion. There was about him that air of command that told Jubal the man had carved an empire from the prairie – or, rather, his father had carved the empire and now the son had inherited the wealth and power.

He gestured with a quirt.

'Go git him, Bill.'

The man who had to be the ramrod dismounted and strode up the steps into the McEnery House. The punchers formed a semicircle, waiting, leaning on their pommels. The sun grew in strength towards mid-morning. People began to move about the streets again, a little puzzled by the Hissing S men's actions, but thankful they were not shooting the town up as usual.

Bill appeared in the door and with him came Dolman. The saloon owner wore no hat and as he stepped down into the street a fresh scratch glittered lividly across his cheek.

So Izah had got in one good clawing before she'd been battered.

Jubal felt convinced Jess Hawken had not seen Dolman. He figured had the old gunslinger done so, Dolman wouldn't be walking forward so jauntily, smiling up at Abe Stoppard, harsh and erect in the saddle.

Stoppard's thickly-coated silver rig gleamed in the sunlight. His black hat threw deep shadows across his face; but Jubal saw the thrust of his jaw, and the way he sat his white stallion, erect, his frock-coated back straight.

'He ain't here, Mr Stoppard.' Dolman spread his hands. 'Had breakfast and then stepped out for a space, I guess.'

'I want him, Dolman. You just find him – fast.'

'Yes, Mr Stoppard, sir.'

Dolman turned, clearly at a loss, ready to call to Sid and the barkeeps to turn out in a town hunt for Doctor Jubal Cade.

A small figure ran from the side alley. Jubal saw the sun glint on wire-framed spectacles. The man held an oily rag. He stood looking up at Stoppard, and his quick words were just a mumble to Jubal, hidden in the shadows of the man's porch.

Jubal licked his lips. He hitched his shoulder rig around. A dozen cowpokes, and of that dozen he figured at least four, maybe five, to be gunhands.

The gunsmith had sneaked out his back door and run across the backlots to the alley siding the McEnery House. Jubal supposed you had to expect that sort of thing in a town owned and run by one man. The tension he felt had to be relieved – the sound of footsteps on the boardwalk snapped his head around.

Sheriff Gil Lovesay walked up towards him, his hand on his gunbutt, his face scowling.

'Figured you'd show up, Doc,' he greeted.

'On my way to see you. Get the story straight.'

'Story you'll have to tell Mr Stoppard.' Lovesay jerked his head towards the group sitting their horses in the sunlight.

'I guess,' allowed Jubal.

As Lovesay stepped into the street, Jubal fell in beside him. The ramrod, Bill, and a couple of other punchers heeled their horses down towards the gunsmith's.

Lovesay held up his left hand.

'He's here,' he called.

Jubal was aware of the slow turn of Abe Stoppard's heavy-set body, the twist of his head as he peered down the street. The rancher wore fancy pearl-handled Colts, saturated with engraving, a pair of guns of great value. The Winchester stuck down

88

the scabbard was likewise heavily engraved. His whole appearance conveyed wealth and power and the knowledge that he had an unlimited quantity of both at his disposal.

'Don't look much,' said Abe Stoppard.

Jubal held quiet. Let them talk it out first. If one of the gunhands started a play, there'd be little chance for him. But with the Sheriff there, the legality of Stoppard's proceedings ought to be seen to be believed. Ought to be ... Jubal put no great store of faith in Sheriff Lovesay's ability to uphold any law other than Stoppard's law in Rawson.

The punchers were looking at the saloon through the windows of the McEnery House and licking their lips. Jubal set himself for a swift leap at Stoppard. He'd point his Colt at the man's head and dare any of them to try to blast him.

'They tell me you're a doc. That right?'

'That's right.'

'Got a medical bag?'

'Yes.'

'Go git it. Bill – go with him. You're riding out with us.'

'My horse is in the livery.'

Stoppard did not look at anyone in particular as he spoke.

'Go git his hoss.'

A man heeled out of the line, cantered off to the livery.

'What you waiting fer, Doc? Bill don't like to be kept waiting.'

'Any reason I should go with you, Stoppard?'

At this a pleased smile split Bill's stubbled face. He hunched his shoulders and flexed his hands. 'Want I should convince him, Mr Stoppard?'

'I don't want him hurt none. Want him in good shape.'

'Gather you require my medical services, Stoppard?'

'Kinda. It's urgent. We'll talk about Jed and Clay after. Now git yore medical bag afore Bill loses what little patience he has.'

Jubal nodded his head and went inside. Bill dismounted again, flinging the reins to his nearest man, and followed Jubal. Bill wore a dark blue shirt, and dark blue pants, with a wide black belt liberally studded with silver. He affected two guns,

Colts, hung low. He walked with a swing and as he walked so he jingled.

His freckled face wore that blank, apparently good-natured, stare that indicated to Jubal a quick readiness to take orders from his boss and to kill without hesitation. These open-faced hombres were often worse than the tight, taut, dark-featured killers.

In his room Jubal hefted his valise. He picked up the Spencer. A click sounded and a Colt showed in Bill's hand. He leered, his thick lips splitting again in that blank, friendly grin.

'You wanta be right careful with that there gun, doc.'

'Oh, I'm always careful of things that take care of me.'

He tucked the Spencer under his arm and caught up his saddle-bags. He was all packed. They clumped down the stairs, with Bill's spurs sounding like bells as they jangled against the boards. Jubal was not fooled by the fancy rig. The speed of the ramrod's draw had convinced him. And no prizes were offered for a guess as to why a rancher should need so many gunhands on his spread. Rawson had to be kept in line.

His bay was there and Seth had taken good care of it. He mounted up and stuck the rifle down the scabbard. He saw the sour expressions on the punchers' faces and guessed they had been herded off from the saloon. He caught the tail of Stoppard's vicious, whip-cracking words.

'Sure we had a long ride and sure we started real early. But we're riding back and we're riding hard. There's no time to waste. I don't want half-drunk bums riding in back of me.' Stoppard stared around the half-circle of men. 'Any o' you wanta take a drink, step right down and belly up to the bar. But iffen you do, don't come crawling back to the Hissing S.'

Not a cowpoke moved.

'Right. You all set, doc? Move out!'

With a staccato rattle of hooves on the parched ground and a clinking of harness, the group wheeled out and started down Rawson's mainstreet riding a line of dust.

The real power that Stoppard wielded had manifested itself in his denial of these thirsty men. A man could cultivate a real fine and dandy thirst riding the range. Any man who could stop him using that thirst for what God intended thirsts to be used for was indeed a man to be reckoned with.

They rode in a tight bunch, knee to knee, out of Rawson and along the trail. Before they reached the climb along Medicine Bluff they hauled out and struck across country. The men fanned out and with horses on a loose rein, legs long in the stirrups, they settled down for the long pull out to the Hissing S.

Once, Jubal had had ideas about setting up as a doctor in Laredo. He had, in the old days when he and Mary were first married, fancied he'd be a hard-working frontier doc, a medical valise and a horse and buggy always at hand, and with his rifle to hand, also; though he had not expected to use it overmuch. The grim reality had been the reverse; he had used the Spencer far more than he had the medical valise.

The group high-tailed it over a long uphill climb and past a few stands of straggling timber, heading away from the vast expanse of the plains. This was good stock country. They dipped down a long reverse slope and broke through a straggle of brush and so hit the main trail out of Rawson, their corner-cutting knocking three hours off the time a team would take. Dust spurted as they rode and hung in a long ochre banner astern of them.

Around midday Stoppard called a halt. The men watered their horses sparingly. Jubal used his derby and, when his horse had drunk what he allowed him, he clapped the derby back on, relishing the cool feel of the water-soaked hat against his head.

'Time to go,' announced Stoppard.

There were a few groans and moans, but the men mounted up dutifully enough and heeled out after the black, erect form of the rancher. By this time Jubal was left to ride as he wished, and so kept well up out of the drag position. He didn't see why he had to eat dust.

They were just looking forward to riding up out of a narrow draw when the first rifle shot blasted the rear rider from his saddle. He went up in the air, shrieking, his guts spewing blood as he tangled his stirrups and fell. His mount, maddened by the smell of blood and the sudden thwack of a bullet past his muzzle, reared and pranced, then lit out in a dead run for the end of the draw. He was allowed to go. The riflemen among the boulders fringing the lip of the draw held their fire on the men and horses milling in roiling clouds of dust below. Slugs ripped through flesh and smashed into bone. Blood spouted, steaming on to the dust.

Jubal heeled his horse over into the side of the draw, riding low, his whole body crouched, ready to slide and hit the ground the moment he got in among the loose scatter of rocks littered along the inner edge of the draw.

A horse reared before him, its rider shrieking, his face a mask of blood. The slug had struck him across the bridge of the nose, shattering the left cheekbone, and exited taking with it most of the left side of his face. The cowpoke screamed and his mouth shed shards of bone and gobbets of blood.

Jubal's bay reared. The bullet that would have scrambled his brains whipped harmlessly past his chest. With a ferocious pull on the reins and a vicious kick with his spurs, Jubal got the beast under control and hammered him hard for the rocks. Dust boiled as another rider went over, his horse kicking and threshing madly, blood staining the black hide.

Out of the corner of his eye Jubal spotted a white horse kicking and rearing, his rider desperately attempting to bring him under control. Either stay on and ride for cover, or get off and duck – that was the style in this ambush.

And Abe Stoppard's beautiful horse was rearing and slashing about with his forehooves so that the rancher could neither dismount nor ride for the rocks.

In that second a bullet cut into the white stallion's neck. Blood spouted as a main artery was severed. Stoppard was yelling as his men pounded past. The dust clamped down and Stoppard's horse crashed over sideways.

Stoppard scrambled free. He stood, shaking, a revolver in his hand firing and firing up at the cliffs until all six chambers had emptied.

Jubal stretched out his right hand, grabbing for Stoppard.

The rancher saw him. His savage face showed a merciless

anger, and, also, a confused inability to understand how he could be bushwhacked on his own land.

Jubal yelled, bending low, sweeping on towards the rancher with the empty Colt in his fist.

'Grab your rifle!'

Dazed, Stoppard gaped.

Jubal hauled his sweating horse up, feeling rather than hearing the wicked crack of bullets as the men up on the lip of the gulch poured their fire in. He landed on his feet and ran, gripping the reins with his left hand.

'Your rifle, you idiot!'

Stoppard heard. He whirled to the kicking horse and yanked the Winchester from the scabbard.

Then Jubal hit him and threw him onto the horse. Now both men lay half-straddled across the saddle, tangled up in the guns and saddlebags and Jubal's valise. Digging in his heels Jubal headed the horse across the remaining open stretch into the harsh light and shade of the rock-strewn edge of the draw.

Bullets cracked off the rocks and cannoned away with shrill ricochets.

Jubal leapt from the horse and grabbed the Spencer out of its scabbard. Then he ripped the valise free of its straps.

Rolling in a head-over-heels flurry of motion, Jubal sledged solidly into a rock. The breath was knocked from his body but he kept his grip on the rifle and the valise. Around him men were sliding in smoky confusion into positions among the boulders.

One did not make it.

Even as Jubal flipped around a boulder and hunkered down, he saw the cowpoke, his face strained and sweat-stained, his eyes blank with shock, jumping for the rocks.

The heavy-calibre rifle bullet hit him just under the right shoulder-blade.

He ran on for a few steps, his mouth open, gurgling, his arms uplifted to the sky as though pleading to the Almighty for help.

The slug exited from his chest in a massive fountain of blood. The whole front of his checked shirt disintegrated as the blood pumped out, and shards of splintered bone glittered in the pink-frothed spray.

He hit the dirt face first a yard from Jubal.

A voice said in Jubal's ear: 'Thet was a .52 calibree Sharps. Yessir. Fair knocks a man's insides out, th' ole Sharps.'

'Yeah,' was all Jubal said. He had experience of the Sharps rifle and knew its capacity for long-range accurate destruction.

The rifle fire continued from above, but now the shots cracked in aimlessly as the shooters above sought targets among the boulders. The loose horses milled and then galloped off to stand shivering some way along the draw, as though momentarily expecting dead riders to strut up spurs jingling, to mount them again.

Still clutching his Spencer and valise, Jubal slid down into the shadow of the boulder. He tipped his derby back, and rested his back against the rock which struck cooler in the shade than the blistering trail out in the centre of the gulch. He turned his head and surveyed the speaker.

He had noticed the man before among Stoppard's riders only because he was the oldest. He wore a patched pair of denims, a shirt that had once been red but was now bleached to the fine pink of an old brick wall. His black hat was so crushed, dented, notched and generally stamped on that it seemed glued to his head. His thin face showed a stubble of white around the jaws, but his eyes were a piercing bright blue and his gnarled brown hands gripped a Henry rifle as though he knew how to use it. Like Jubal, and unlike many of the younger cowpokes and gun-hands, he had made no attempt to shoot blindly back at the lip of the gulch.

'Name's Hank, doc,' he said, speaking around a chaw of tobacco. 'Reckon you'll git yore hand in soon, perfessional, like.'

'Likely.'

'These young gunsels, reckon they c'n ride and shoot like the prairee's afire ahint 'em. They give me the belly laughs, they sure do – if I wuzn't too old fer laffin.'

Jubal smiled. He did not say, 'You and Jess Hawken, too.' But the thought was there.

They crouched in the lee of the boulder as bullets cracked and smacked and smeared lead above them. A puncher screamed as he levered up to shoot, and fell back, that sound his last on earth. His head was taken off, exposing the brains, and blood flowed down around his face like a bizarre and horrifying hairstyle. He collapsed, kicking with stiffening legs, and lay still.

'Never larn, these punks,' opined Hank.

'How come you're riding with them?'

'Guess that's a good question, son. But somebody has to look out fer the boss. Young Abe's a mighty headstrong feller. He feels the blood in his veins. A mighty big man, now, young Abe.'

That clued Jubal into the picture.

He settled his shoulders more comfortably and put the valise down carefully. So far the men hit by the Sharps up there hadn't lived. A few Winchesters had fired, also, and in a lull in the shooting Jubal called to see if any of the trapped men were wounded and needed assistance. When a weak cry came from the boulders about ten yards to his left he picked up his valise, jammed his derby on hard, and hefted the Spencer.

'Keep yore haid down, doc. I ain't had the luxuree o' a real live sawbones in a fight with me afore.'

'If you're hit,' promised Jubal. 'I'll doctor you real proud.'

'Glad to hear it, doc.'

The puncher held up a blood-soaked arm. The Winchester .44 had gone clean through the fleshy part. Jubal patched him up and then said: 'When we break out, you can still shoot.'

'Have a heart, doc – I'm wounded!'

He was young, with the fancy rig of the puncher who had learned to handle a gun and fancied himself king of the mountain. His sallow face sweated and he kept on swallowing.

'You'll shoot when it comes to it,' advised Jubal and wriggled back to Hank. There were things he wanted to know. Things, he told himself severely, that he merely wanted to know for the sake of his own survival. He had no intention of embroiling himself in the family feuds of the Stoppards and the Pattersons and the Hawkens – of Jess Hawken rather, for the old gunslinger was a loner.

95

When he got back, the gunfire from above went on but in a lower key, as though the bushwhackers had all day in which to flush their game. He found Abe Stoppard talking with Hank.

Stoppard's heavy face was still flushed with the anger he never bothered to control. He held a fancy Winchester with the engraved frame depicting a hunting scene of bears and lavish scrollwork surrounding the central cartouche. A bullet spanged off the boulder and chips of rock rained down. The Winchester in Stoppard's hands shook, but Jubal could quite clearly see the man was tense with anger and disbelieving rage, not fear.

'I'll have me them! I'll have 'em drawn and scattered for the buzzards!'

'Them ain't injuns, young Abe,' opined Hank, and he spat a long straw-yellow stream that hit a fly dead centre. The fly fell off the rock and drowned in a rapidly evaporating pool.

'I know they're not Injuns, you goddam old fool!'

Jubal plunked the valise down and stilled.

'Who do you reckon they are?'

Hank cackled at that. 'One guess,' he said, before Stoppard could get the bitter words out. 'One guess ain't one too many. Hell, no.'

'All right, Hank, all right. So the Croxley Boys hev come back. But this time I'll dismember 'em all, every last one.'

Instantly, Jubal's passions were fully engaged.

He swung to face Stoppard. His thin face with the pallid scar tissue glittering over the bridge of his nose drove the big rancher back in sudden shock.

'You sure it's the Croxley gang?'

'Hey, doc – you sure look mean—'

'Is it?'

Stoppard abruptly realized just who he was. The horror of the ambush must have temporarily driven a great deal from his mind. Now he fronted Jubal in the shadow of the boulder.

'You watch your tongue, doc. I need you. But you talk outta turn—'

Jubal interrupted, speaking with a fierce, hating passion.

'Hank reckons it's the Croxley Boys. Do you?'

'Yeah. Ain't no one but them fool enough to tangle with me on Hissing S territory.'

Jubal let his tense body relax. He could feel the tremble in him and he fought it. He would need a steady hand on the trigger and a mercilessly steady eye behind the backsight of the Spencer.

'D'you happen to know a guy with a scar—' Here Jubal made the fierce gesture across his forehead he had made so many times without any luck. 'Lee Kincaid—'

'That rattler! I'd as soon blast him as pass the time of day.'

'Well, Stoppard. Don't. Leave him to me. Or I'd as soon blast the man who gets him first.'

Stoppard caught his breath. 'I believe you, doc – but—?'

A bullet spanged from the boulder and Hank spat with practised accuracy at the spot where the ricochet hit up dust.

'Seems they aim to keep us here 'til dark,' he said.

A man's voice knifed down from above, cutting through the rifle din. Instantly every rifle fell silent. A dead silence fell over the dry gulch. Stoppard looked up. Then he started to rise.

'Don't,' said Jubal.

Stoppard looked sideways, his eyes two gleaming crescents of hatred.

Hank said swiftly, 'Reckon that makes sense, young Abe.'

'Bushwhacking me on my own land, and a dude kid doctor telling me what to do—'

'It's just not your day, is it, Stoppard?'

The thudding hoofbeats and the rattling of iron-rimmed wheels heralded a new interruption. Jubal levered around and peered slantwise under the curve of the boulder. He could see along the edge of the gulch and out along the trail aways. Pretty soon, as the sounds of the coach drew nearer, he saw the lifting plume of dust and then the Stetson-crowned heads of the driver and shotgun and then the hard outline of the coach. When the horses' heads broke into view over the crest in the trail they were dangerously close, blowing hard, bearing down fast on him.

'So that's it!' he exclaimed.

He lifted the Spencer and triggered three quick shots.

'Doubt they'll hear, son,' said Hank.

But it was too late. It had been too late from the moment the stagecoach thundered over the crest. A fusillade of shots broke from the boulders above the trail. Two horses went down, kicking and screaming. The others piled on to their team mates. The coach swerved drunkenly. The driver pitched out, trailing the reins, and the shotgun guard made a frantic grab for the rail at his side. He missed.

Driver and guard fell headlong from the coach. It swerved again and crashed into the wheel horses. A cloud of dust spurted. The wheels hit the loose rocks. The Concord tilted over and smashed full onto its side, skidding amidst the dirt and dust for twenty yards. Then it came to a stop, its upper wheels still revolving.

'So that's what the bastards was after,' said Stoppard.

'She's due in Rawson just afore sundown. Reckon the stage'll be late today.' And Hank pursed and spat, another shot on his target.

Movement showed at the upturned side windows of the coach. A rattle of gunfire broke the eerie silence and the movement ceased.

'If them fools try to git out!'

'There's silver in that coach,' said Stoppard. 'I know. Fifty per cent of it is mine.'

'Well,' Jubal told him, 'you're lucky you're here to protect your property.'

'I'm here because my fool boy got hisself a busted leg and arm tangling with barbed wire—'

'That's what he says.' Hank chewed, and then pointedly looked off at the coach, which was just visible past the end of the boulder. Above them the gulch's cliff-like rise protected them from an overhead shot and the boulder shielded them from fire from the other lip.

'You hesh up, Hank. You dunno what happened.'

'I c'n guess, tho'.'

'He wasn't drunk. Jim don't drink that much.'

Hank screwed his eyes up. 'I saw the way his face was cut up.

That weren't no barbed wire. Leastways, no barbed wire I ever did see. An' I ain't seed much, glory be.'

'So it's your son Jim who needs my attention?' Jubal did not take his eyes off the overturned coach. He had seen the quick flash of the sun on metal. Pretty soon the whole draw would be in shadow. But if whoever was in the coach decided to make a break for it, he'd be lucky to cover two yards with those marksmen atop the cliff.

'Yeah. Broke his arm and leg. And got cut about the face and chest. Barbed wire – figure they ought to shoot the cuss invented it. Shoot him down like a coyote.'

Jubal switched his gaze back from the coach and tried to squint up to the nearest point of the rocky lip. He didn't fancy sticking his neck out. He licked his lips and wished he had the canteen strapped to the bay.

'Stalemate,' he said. 'Croxley's Boys have the silver in the coach waiting for them to come down and pick it up. But we're down here ready to blast 'em the moment they make their move.'

Stoppard brightened.

'Hey, that's right! Iffen they try for the coach we'll cut 'em to pieces.'

'It's gonna be a long wait,' opined Hank, groaning.

'They didn't expect anybody to be in this area at this time,' reasoned Jubal. 'You rode into town and rode out again pretty fast. They couldn't have anticipated that.'

'Yeah. If it wasn't fer—' Here Hank glanced at the boulder face, meaning to indicate the dead men. 'If it weren't for them I'd be laffin fit to bust a gut.'

Movement was possible among the scattered boulders, although no one particularly wanted to go sashaying around. When Bill wriggled into the cover of the boulder sheltering Jubal, the ramrod's face was sheened with sweat.

Dust stained his fancy blue outfit.

'What's the next move, boss? We gonna stay here 'till night?'

It would grow cold, then, when the sun went down. Very cold.

'If you wanta go for a mosey along the trail, Bill, you're sure welcome to try.'

'No offence, boss. Just askin', just askin'.'

There was no way up the cliffs at their backs that Jubal could see. A monkey or a mountain goat might manage it. To expose any part of a man's anatomy would draw down a murderous fire. Again there was movement at the coach window. This time the big Sharps sent their .52 bullets cracking into the woodwork. Maybe the load was the government .50-70 cartridge. Either way, the movement stopped and a muffled howl broke across the dusty gulch.

'Dang fool,' said Hank, spitting.

'How many Sharps do you figure, Hank? How many repeaters?'

'Been tryin' to figger that out meself.' Hank screwed up his weatherbeaten eyes until they all but disappeared in harsh folds of sere brown flesh. His whiskery jowls continued to rotate as he chewed. 'Seems to me there's two dang good Sharps boys up there, and mebbe three more with repeaters. Otherwise they'd have riddled the coach clear through.'

'There are more than five men up there!' exclaimed Stoppard, wrathfully. 'I wouldn't be stuck down here against five men, no matter how good they were.'

'They hold all the aces, Stoppard,' said Jubal. 'But I figure four with repeaters – I fancy there's a Spencer up there.'

Jubal let the oldster say it, out of amusement.

'Course,' said Hank, chewing and speaking with great enjoyment. 'That's on'y on that side. Half a dozen more o' the varmints this side, over atop our haids.'

'Oh,' said Abe Stoppard, and he swallowed.

Abruptly, with a roaring crash like the end of the world, a massive boulder tumbled down from the lip of the gulch. It hit among the rocks below and exploded like a howitzer shell. Razor-sharp stone splinters scissored through the air. Jubal hit dirt and felt the sliding impact of a stone sliver go razoring past his left ear. A man screamed. Almost instantly another boulder plummeted down.

Jubal lifted up, not much, but enough.

'Get back!' he bellowed. 'Under the overhang.'

The men held low and skittering like skaters went sliding and sprawling back away from the first boulders to the safety of those close up under the cliff edge. After a moment the boulders ceased to fall.

The screaming man was dragged over to Jubal, who bent to examine him.

'The dirty scheming varmints—' Hank was saying.

'Hesh up, you old fool!' said Stoppard. 'Listen. And keep Charlie quiet, for God's sake!'

Jubal put a hand to Charlie's mouth, looking into his eyes.

'Hold it for a spell, son – I'll give you something for the pain directly.'

Stoppard was listening with a fierce expression plastered over his savage features.

A man shouted, high and shrill, and laughter followed. Then came the sound of boots sliding in dusty rock crevices.

'Scream, Charlie,' said Jubal.

Charlie let rip a tremendous bellow of sound. Everyone looked up. The shadows dropped over the scene in the draw. The sound of men breathing in harsh ragged gasps punctuated Charlie's yells. Jubal let off a couple of realistic groans, tailing them away, giving an artistic performance of a badly wounded man expiring.

Charlie's left ear had been near-enough ripped off. Drenched with blood it hung askew. Jubal took it in his fingers and rammed it back, holding it there whilst he rapidly layered a bandage.

'I'll sew it on real fancy when I get time, Charlie.'

'Thanks, doc—'

'Don't thank me. Start screaming.'

Hank let out a bellow, and then groaned, working his chops around his chaw. He was thoroughly enjoying himself.

'What fool's game is this?' demanded Stoppard. 'Shut that damnfool yowling, Hank!'

'They'll think they've got three of us, Stoppard,' Jubal pointed out. 'It's getting dark, and cold. They'll be down soon – and they'll come shooting.'

The temperature dropped with that frightening speed that could destroy an unprepared man. If they didn't get to move around pretty soon and keep their circulations going they'd freeze. Jubal set his jaws tightly and then forced himself to relax. The scraping noises came again. The shadows grew deeper and gloomier. The stars began to prick out in the velvety blue above. The cold struck in.

Jubal picked up the Colt abandoned by a dead man and checked the load. It had been fired empty. Maybe that was why the man was dead. With fingers that felt the chill of the metal he loaded up, the fat .45 cartridges sliding in, the cylinder snapping shut with a sharp, satisfying clunk, loud in the cold shadows of the gulch. Up above there would still be a little grey light remaining, down here the shadows pressed in.

Stuffing the spare gun into his belt, Jubal half-rose into a crouch. He peered cautiously around the side of the big boulder. At his side Hanks breathed wheezily.

'See anythin', doc?'

'No.'

'They're a-coming down. Thet's fer sure.'

'Yes.'

Stoppard felt renewed anxiety about his son. He pushed up in back of Jubal, his anger still burning inside, giving him a vicious cutting edge. 'Hank set Jim's arm and leg, doc. But it's his insides I'm worried about. He was busted up inside.'

'Falling off his horse in barbed wire?'

'Yes.'

Hank said nothing, but his angular figure stiffened in the gloom.

'The quicker we get to the Hissing S the better, then.' Jubal half-turned to the dim form of Hank. 'You fix him up real good, Hank?'

'Purty good,' Hank allowed. 'Hafta splint laigs and arms when there's no doc around. Nothing to it.'

Frontier medicine might be weak in many areas, setting fractured bones, if the fractures were not too complicated, was an art well within the competence of old hands like Hank.

Jubal edged forward. The Spencer in his left hand snaked out. He hefted his valise.

'Hell, doc,' exploded Hank. 'I'm a-coming with you!'

'You stay here, Hank,' snapped Stoppard.

'I c'n doctor real good—'

'Stay here, you old fool, and let the young 'uns do the fighting.' Stoppard spoke in his mean voice.

'Now, lissen here, young Abe. Many's the time I've bathed you and potted you and tied up your—'

'Hank!'

The oldster subsided, fuming and grumbling to himself. The hissing sound followed by the juicy splat of tobacco juice hitting rock told them all just how he felt. But he pulled back, deeper into the shadows.

'Take care o' yore bag, doc. Jist make sure you gits back here in one piece.'

'If your hide gets perforated I'll be back to doctor you,' Jubal told him. 'Although I'm not saying I won't bill you for services rendered.'

Hank groaned. 'Ain't nuthin' free no more.'

Jubal took a grip on the Spencer and on the valise, the twin symbols of his life in the West, and, like a prowling timberwolf, slid out into the deadly shadows of the gulch.

CHAPTER NINE

There had been four passengers travelling in the stage.

Three of them were dead, still dark forms sprawled against the windows and door, with the dust sifted in through the smashed windows already settling on their bodies. Jubal wriggled over the upturned stage and froze as a thick, slurred voice said tiredly: 'Just a little further, and I'll take your head off.'

'Hold steady, friend,' said Jubal in a still whisper. 'I'm a doctor.'

'Now I've heard it all.' The tired, slurred voice broke into a harsh cackle. 'Fred! Abe! Luke! To th'sside – action left flank! The blue-bellies are acoming in – see them black hats—' The voice mumbled away incoherently.

Jubal eased over the shattered door and dropped down. It was pitch dark in the stage and he trod on soft squashy things before he found a secure purchase against an upright. He bent to the feebly moving form. Working by touch he established the man had been hit in the upper arm. Winchester .44, probably, judging by the damage to the humerus. Had the slug been fired from a Sharps .52 the humerus would have been shattered and probably the scapula and clavicle would have been wrenched into ruin with it. Jubal got busy.

The man moaned.

'Hold still, friend. Have you fixed up in two shakes.'

His own movements were sure, deft, quick with the need for silence and compassion. He strained his ears to pick up what was going on out there along the trail beneath the cliffs. He barely had time to finish patching the soldier up. He drew the dark blue coat back over the strapped arm, guessing the colour, knowing this man had fought wearing a uniform of grey or butternut, easing him into a more comfortable position.

Three shots rang out in quick succession.

A whoop followed – a signal, not the cry of a wounded man.

Jubal placed his valise down carefully, avoiding the congealed blood splashed over the stage and eased the Spencer up. He wriggled over the shattered side of the Concord like a rattler, his eyes adjusted to the star-shot gloom, already picking out moving targets from passive boulders.

The Croxley Boys were prowling in like coyotes to take the silver and high tail it out of there. They'd have a hideaway somewhere close, some place where they could feel safe, a place similar to the Patterson homestead they had raided last time – nine months ago.

A voice hissed close by.

'Keep your head down, Tom, you danged idjit.'

And the rejoinder, 'Keep your arse down, Charley, you galoot.'

They would be Tom and Charley Croxley, two of one-eyed Zeke Croxley's sons. The father and the other son, Rube, would be out there, guns at the ready. With them would be Smiling Leefe and – and, Jubal prayed, his fists gripped around the Spencer – and Lee Kincaid.

More gunshots broke the furtive silence of the night.

A man screamed. This time the shriek ripped from a raw throat, torn by the blasting impact of a bullet ripping flesh and smashing bone.

A fusillade broke out. Bullets spanged and cracked on either side of Jubal, hitting the coach, and he cursed and dived for the rocky ground. He hit and rolled over, the Spencer coming up pointed at dark shapes which moved in on him.

He held his fire.

They could be Stoppard's men just as easily as Croxley's.

Moving cautiously, head down, his eyes raking the dimness, Jubal moved out. He circled. He came up in back of one man who was crawling towards the overturned stage.

Bullets slammed through the night and another man let out a choked yell. The fight was a crazy muddled affair, with men trying to keep their enemies in sight and not get shot by their own side. Jubal put the Spencer muzzle against the man's neck and pushed – hard.

'Roll over, gently.'

The man dropped his rifle and rolled. His face showed two black pits for eyes and a shadow-haunted face, sweat glinting in the starlight. It was now possible for Jubal to make out details with fair clarity, the clear clean atmosphere laid no obstruction to the night sky.

He was not one of Stoppard's men.

He was not Lee Kincaid.

He tried to play it clever and, rolling, tried to claw past the Spencer muzzle and draw his pistol.

Jubal shot him.

The slug smashed through his neck, releasing a welling tide of black liquid. No scream could burst past the shattered larynx.

Even as he shot and witnessed the effect of his shot, Jubal powered himself sideways and rolled.

Bullets hammered into the ground. Some slugged into the body of the man. He twitched and jumped under the repeated impacts.

There were some careless gunmen out there this night. The Croxley boys would shoot at anything that moved, not giving a damn for anything but their own skins. Only Stoppard's men might try to ascertain who it was they were firing at and now, revising his first ideas on the muddled fight, Jubal began to wonder if they'd care over much, either.

A man reared up in the starlight, flinging forward, aiming to drop on top of Jubal. Starlight glinted along the blade of a wicked Bowie.

Jubal rolled and came up on to a knee, levering the Spencer. The hammer fell and the gun belched fire. Instantly, as he had before, Jubal powered away. This second man died under a rain of bullets fired by friend and foe alike. They were shooting at anything that moved. They were shooting at any blast of gunfire out there. Jubal prowled on. Two down. How many more to go?

He hunkered down beside a boulder, staring meanly out across the starlit expanse. His old grey derby looked just like a boulder. He saw a sharply-pointed rock a dozen yards off, a rock that was moving gently. Stetsons were nowhere when it came to imitating landscape. The derby served admirably.

Jubal eased along, careful to make no noise, conscious that as a city-bred youngster he should stand no chance against these range-riders. But they were not animated by the burning passions of Jubal Cade. They were not seeking to find the murderer who had killed a wife and shattered a dream – and who had also turned a doctor into a killer.

Jubal tossed a stone off to the right. Stetson jerked that way and his Colt came up. He did not fire. Easing into position, Jubal pointed the Spencer at Stetson's head and said evenly, 'Just put the gun down nice and easy.'

Stetson fancied his luck. He dived and rolled and swung the Colt around in a quick-handed flip, pulling the trigger as he hit.

The Spencer flamed once. Stetson's bullet cracked off to smack into the cliff. Jubal skidded sideways, hunkering down, and the expected blast of fire tore the air in his last position. Stetson screeched once and then flopped back, riddled and shredded.

Three down.

Not one was the scar-faced killer. Kincaid liked to kill. He'd be sitting out there cheerfully sending his shots to smash into whoever received them, not giving a damn, waiting until there was no answering fire before sauntering over to the stage and taking the silver. Jubal's rage seethed inside him. His lips thinned out and he felt the skin across his forehead and cheeks grow tight with the anger. His eyes blazed, and across the bridge of his nose, white scar tissue showed pale in the starlight.

He spotted another man creeping cautiously forward. The dark clothes told him nothing. Moving with stealth, Jubal got into position. He lifted the Spencer.

'Hold steady, feller. Put the gun down.'

The man stopped abruptly. He turned around, dropping his revolver.

'Hell, doc! You kinda give a man a shock.'

It was the ramrod, Bill. He scooped his gun up.

'What in hell's going on? You seen any o' the Croxley Boys?' Bill looked mean and angry.

'Some. Where's Stoppard?'

'Out at the far end o' the gulch.' An abrupt burst of fire from there underlined Bill's words.

Hunkering down, Jubal took fresh shells from his vest pocket and reloaded the Spencer.

'Reckon he's kinda figuring on leavin', doc. He's more worried about his boy than the silver.'

'There's a wounded man in the stage. Got to get him out safely.'

'To hell with him! When the boss says move, you move.'

Jubal looked down the muzzle of the ramrod's Colt.

He took a breath. He could feel the sweat icy on him.

'You going to use that thing, Bill?'

'If I have to.'

'Can't tend Stoppard's son with a slug in me.'

'Where I'll shoot yuh, won't make no difference.'

The foreman was not bluffing. His finger tightened on the trigger.

Somewhere in the dimness about him Lee Kincaid was sitting, hidden up behind a boulder, shooting at targets and loving his work. Jubal was not prepared to leave.

'Put thet rifle down, doc. Nice and easy. Finger away from the trigger.'

An abrupt crescendo of shots broke from the far end of the draw. A raking spread of fire that sent bullets cracking and spanging about Jubal and Stoppard's foreman. Both men hit the dirt, rolling into the cover of the rocks. The massed gunfire smashed down the gulch, enveloping the whole area in the savage concussions of battle.

Men were yelling and shrieking. Horses screamed, whinnying their fear. The stink of burnt powder hung in the air.

A form flitted in front of Jubal, running from left to right. Too fast for a shot.

Voices yelled, and then among the bedlam a harsh, croaking, bad-tempered voice hollered above the din.

'Git yo' hosses! Ain't no good fightin' a whole army!'

Boot soles scraped rock. The shooting bellowing down the drift reached giant proportions and then began to tail away.

Horses whinnied and the sound of hooves battering the dirt racketed up from the opposite end of the gulch.

Jubal raised a cautious head. He still held the Spencer.

Bill stared up with a frozen grin etched across his lips.

'Guess Mrs Stoppard got tired waiting for the boss to git home.'

The riders who had burst onto the scene and so radically changed the picture hauled their mounts up. There were curses and yells and good-natured greetings. More than one horse would have been brought down in the confusing star-shot darkness. Two pistol shots emphasized that, putting an end to the animals' pain.

Stoppard strode out, the fancy silver of his rig catching the starlight and glittering. He stood looking up at the lead rider, and something about his stance indicated very clearly that the men of the Hissing S might call him the boss, but the woman who sat regarding him with a fierce and bitter scorn was the real boss – and didn't mind who knew it.

'Why, Candice – you shouldn't'a come riding in like that! You could'a got yourself shot.'

'No thanks to you if'n I did, Abe. Now git mounted up and let's get out of here. Ain't no sense in riding after them Croxley Boys in the dark. Hurry, now!'

'Yes, Candice,' said Abe Stoppard.

Hank appeared leading his own horse, a mouldy-looking grey that concealed stamina beneath her mangy appearance. The other horses trailed up, their hooves clattering. The cowpokes set about collecting their mounts. Not all the ponies remained alive, but there were enough mounts. The dead men accounted for that. Jubal pushed through and saw that Charlie's ear was still bandaged. Then he turned his attention to Stoppard.

The rancher sat a black gelding, his head half-tilted, listening to his wife chewing him out.

'And tell that ramrod o' yourn to git the silver. Where's this no-good doctor you was supposed to be fetching?'

Jubal stepped forward.

'There's a wounded man in the stage needs attention. If you—'

'You the doc?'

Jubal nodded. The woman was a mere shadow against the stars, but he caught the strong angular presence of her.

'The wounded man's a—'

'I don't give a straw what he is. You git on yore horse and go tend to my Jimmy. Move it out real fast, doc. I cain't abide a man who dilly-dallies about when there's work needs doing.'

There was no sign as yet of Jubal's bay. Horses would naturally tend to stick together and if his mount hadn't showed up with the rest he must presume it to be dead. He ignored the woman and started to walk towards the stage.

'Doc! Hold it right there!'

'Going to fetch my valise,' said Jubal without halting or turning. The rocky ground was treacherous underfoot. 'No good to your boy without.'

'Go git it, then, and quick. Where's your hoss?'

A horse was essential. Jubal half-turned. 'Don't see him around. He must have been shot.'

'Find the doc a hoss, and sharp!' Candice Stoppard's voice rang in the gulch. She would be obeyed. Jubal remembered how Jess Hawken had described her. This was the woman who had run off the Pattersons from her husband's spread, condemned them to a miserable patch of ground and a tumbledown shack.

Shadows clustered thickly about the overturned stage. Reaching down inside, Jubal checked the soldier. His hand encountered the man's face, and he felt down gently under the jaw and on to the neck. The pulse was very weak; but in its hesitant fluttering remained hope for the soldier if he could get proper treatment. Jubal hefted his valise and stepped back.

'Can you fix up a litter for this wounded man?' he called across the intervening stretch of starshot dimness. 'Don't want to leave him—'

'We'll take care of him, doc. Now jest you mount-up and let's ride out. Bill will take care of everything.'

'Yes, Cade,' snapped Abe Stoppard, his heavy voice echoing his wife's shrewish snap. 'Step lively. I'm plumb wore out and I need a drink.'

'Don't we all!' called a cowpoke from the darkness, and there was a rippled grunt of assent from the other hands.

Jubal had no intention of going meekly. He needed that horse. Then he'd put his head down and ride like the wind for the far end of the draw, belting out on the heels of the Croxley gang. With them rode the scar-faced killer. Jubal wasn't going to give up on that bastard so easily – not when he was so close.

He walked back, picking his way over the scattered rocks and bypassing a couple of dead bodies. The horse was a skewbald. He slung his valise up and buckled it down and then put his left foot in the stirrup.

'Hurry it up, doc!'

Without replying, Jubal swung up into the saddle. He gripped the reins with his left hand and stuffed the Spencer down the empty scabbard. He took off his derby and wiped sweat with the back of his hand. It banded his forehead like a tourniquet of ice. Then he stretched up in the stirrups, ready to jam in his heels, let rip with a wild screech, slap his hat down on the horse's rump and take off flying.

He started his move and the gulch fell on his head.

He had time to hear Stoppard's heavy voice, thick with passion, shouting, 'You'd better not have tapped him too hard, Bill, or I'll have your hide.'

Then he was swooping and sliding away down a long black greased chute to nowhere.

CHAPTER TEN

Somewhere a man was screaming, a howling, throat-ripping shriek of pure grief. Terror and horror and disbelief all echoed in that insane wail of hopeless loss.

Andy was dead. Dead as his wife Mary was dead. Dead and gone, his back a blood-drenched horror. Dead and buried with a pitiful marker over his small grave.

Saul Klein might be dead, his white albino skin decorated with his own spilled blood, but Andy Prescott was dead, and that was a thing not to be borne.

Blood and death and destruction; these were the facts of life to Jubal Cade. He had been a doctor with healing in his hands and compassion in his heart – and now he was a killer with death in his fists and merciless vengeance in his heart.

His throat hurt. He was being shaken. He snapped his eyes open. He had been the distant man screaming out his torment and grief to a disinterested world.

Hank stared down at him, a look of confusion mixed with compassion on his face, his white-stubbled jaws working rhythmically.

'Ease up, son. You sure got a right case o' the black dog riding you.'

Jubal struggled to a sitting position. He was on a small truckle bed in a plain room with a single small window. The sun slanted in and he judged it was very early in the morning. His throat hurt from the yelling and his head ached from the gunbutt.

'Bill hit me,' he said. Then, 'Bastard.'

'Had to, son. The missus figured you was getting all set to up stakes and pull out. Now that wouldn't be right, seeing as young Jim needs tending.'

'How is he?'

'Reckon he's nigh as bad as you, doc.'

Hank bustled him out of the little storeroom into the ranch-house where he was half-pushed, half-led out to the porch and onto the yard. Here he washed up, trying not to shake his head too much. A quick survey indicated the house to be substantial, built with style, whitewashed, and situated in a commanding position – just in case hostiles showed up.

Stoppard appeared, looking washed-out.

'That was a plumb fool trick you tried to play, doc. How's your head?'

'Addled.'

'Huh?'

'Where's your boy – Jim? Bring my valise. The quicker I can light out after Croxley.' A thought hit him. 'How's the soldier? And Charlie?'

Stoppard stuck his thumbs into the armholes of his fancy vest. The Albert glittered in the early sun, warm and golden. 'Charlie ain't hearing so good this mornin'. The soldier boy'll live. His arm's clean busted, but it'll mend. Right good work there, doc. You do good work on Jim, you hear?'

'Don't stand gossiping, Stoppard! Go fetch my valise and let me practise!'

Hank ran off at Stoppard's bellow. Together, they went into the ranch house and through the wide, low-ceilinged living-room to Jim's bedroom, a cool corner room to the north east. Here Jubal, taking his valise from Hank, stepped towards the bed. The room was decorated in real ranch-house style, with a pair of bull's horns on the wall, buffalo-hides on the walls, a collection of firearms in a case, spurs and fancy boots and Stetsons slung on the floor. Jubal could not see a single book. He looked down on young Jim Stoppard.

After a thorough inspection, he looked up at Hank.

'You did a fine job on his arm and leg, Hank. Near as I can tell they'll heal out straight. Won't take the splints off. His face'll heal up in time. Looks like a wildcat got him.'

'I told you,' snarled Stoppard. 'Barbed wire.'

'Yes. So you did. Let him sleep until he wakes. Then I'll see about his insides.'

'Thought you said you were in a hurry?'

Jubal shook his head, puzzled. He was in a hurry, a tearing, searing, lung-bursting hurry to get astride a saddle and go riding like fury after the Croxley Boys. But all his professional instincts as a doctor could not be denied. He had to think of his patient first.

'He's resting easy. Sleep's the best medicine until I know more. Anywhere to get a bite to eat around here?'

'Better wake him up, doc. Get doctoring.'

Hank made a deep gurgle in his throat.

'Like I said, Stoppard. You want me to do my work, you let me.' Jubal's examination had shown him the boy was in no immediate danger. If his insides were damaged, he was not spitting blood, and Jubal reasoned that sleep would do half his work for him. He could be wrong, but the look of Jim Stoppard, despite his ravaged face, convinced him he was not.

Hank was looking around desperately for a spittoon.

'Go outside, Hank, you old fool!' snarled Stoppard. 'Then git back in here and stick with Jim.'

'Don't I allus do that, young Abe?' declared Hank, and trotted outside to select a suitable target and let fly.

Jim Stoppard moaned tightly in his sleep and his scratched face, mottled with bruising, crumpled. He was, judged Jubal, going through a bad dream, a touch of Hank's black dog. The boy's face bore little family resemblance to that of Abe Stoppard's; it was tight-pinched, thin about the mouth, angular as to chin and nose. Probably took after his mother. He did not, to Jubal's level gaze, appear a prepossessing individual at all. Yet, one day, he would grow up to inherit the whole Hissing S spread and with it overlordship of Rawson. Jubal judged his age to be around twenty.

Abruptly, Jubal made up his mind. He bent as Jim Stoppard moaned again and tried to thrash from side to side. He held him, and Hank stepped anxiously forward to assist. Jubal took the young man's ear lobe in his lean powerful fingers and pressed. Presently, ceasing to thrash about, Stoppard opened his eyes.

'Wha—?' he started.

'Lie easy son,' advised Jubal. 'Just take it easy. I'm not going to hurt you.'

When Jim Stoppard was fully aware of the situation and Jubal started his fresh examination, this time with the yelps of pain from his patient to give him a much better guide, Jubal was brought into a rapid and harsh understanding of his true position here on the Hissing S spread. Abe Stoppard stepped to the side of the bed where Jubal tried to elicit more informative answers to his enquiries than shouted 'ouches' and 'you bastard, doc', and similar evasions. Jubal looked up at a sharp and ominous click.

Abe Stoppard stood, legs spread, leaning forward, pointing a superb Beaumont-Adams at Jubal's midriff.

'You're hurting my boy, doc. I don't like that—'

'Got to locate the damage inside. Just leave me to get on with my job—'

'And I'm telling you, doc. Any more harm comes to my boy and you get it. Not quick. Kneecaps, groin, like that. You know?'

A drop of sweat trickled from Jubal's nose. He stared down again at Jim Stoppard. 'Does it hurt here?' He pressed.

The Stoppard heir shrieked.

'Thought so,' opined Jubal, stepping back and looking around for his valise.

'I warned you, doc! What you doing?'

'I think your boy is in deep trouble, Stoppard. Whoever gave him the going over dealt him some punishing body blows—'

'I told you!' The Beaumont-Adams shook. 'He tangled with the barbed-wire. He said so hisself—'

'Then it must have been the posts that smashed up his kidneys. Pancreas too, most likely. He'll have to be fed very carefully. Liquids monitored. Rest is essential. I'll apply a bandage and do what I can – but, like I said, those guys used pistol butts as well as boots.'

'What the hell are you talking about – monit-whazzat? Drinks? Hank gave him a bitter-root concoction to make him sleep.' Here Stoppard half-turned. Jubal moved in smoothly, smashed a flat palm against the rancher's forearm with his right hand, took the revolver away with his left. He flipped it in the air, caught the hand-filling butt, feeling the superb balance of the piece, and said in his quiet conversational voice, 'Oh, Hank's patent medicine won't do any harm at this late stage. Sleep and as little use of the kidneys as possible is recommended. And I don't like people pointing guns at me. It makes me nervous.'

Stoppard rubbed his forearm. He glanced at his son in the bed and shook his head. 'No, son—'

Jubal spun and ducked in a single flaming movement.

The revolver shot smashed with obscene power in the room. An earthenware jug shattered and spouted water over the wall. Jubal went on with his rolling dive and finished up in a crouch at the head of the bed. He put the muzzle of the revolver against Jim Stoppard's head.

'You know I don't have to cock this beauty with my thumb, Jim? You know that? You know your paw's favourite gun?'

Jim Stoppard shook. He wet his lips. His father stood waiting, helpless.

'I know,' said Jim.

'That's fine, then. I'll doctor you up real good. If you don't recover – if you do die – it won't be my fault. But I find it riles me to work with guns pointing at me. I'm sure you understand.' He stood up, hefting the Beaumont-Adams, took the still-smoking Colt from Jim's nerveless hand. He skidded the Colt away into the far corner.

'Now, Stoppard. You can have your gun back anytime. I must say I admire your taste.'

'You bastard, doc! I'll—'

'Remember your son! Do I get to working on him, or does he lie there and suffer?'

Stoppard cursed. His heavy face showed that same fierce anger overlaid with concern. 'All right, doc. You win – this time. I'll take my gun now. You have my word you won't be harmed whilst Jim lives.'

Jubal ignored the open threat. By that time he ought to have parlayed an entirely different situation. He flipped the Beaumont-Adams across. As Stoppard took the weapon into his

116

hand, Jubal tensed ready for a lethal spring if the rancher reneged on his word.

Stoppard said, with a sigh: 'She shore is a beautiful piece. Had her made up to shoot Winchester .44's in San Francisco. Spanish gunsmith. Said it was a pleasure and a privilege to work on such an arm. English, the gun is. Cost me a packet.'

'Yes,' said Jubal, bending to Jim and beginning to do what he could for the boy. 'They aren't turned out on a sausage machine, a thousand a time. Each one's made real true.'

'I know. And if you fail me, Doc Cade, you'll get a Winchester .44 shot from this here Beaumont-Adams right through your mangy heart.'

'Hand me that bedsheet, Stoppard.' Jubal snatched it and ripped it into long strips, went on with his binding.

'Anyway,' continued Stoppard, clearly talking to cover his anguish at the condition of his son. 'How'd you know she was my favourite gun?'

'Anybody own a gun like that it'd be their favourite, wouldn't it?'

'In course – yeah.'

Stoppard shifted. He stuck the Beaumont-Adams back into the holster, hawked up spit, looked around, swallowed. 'Ain't said about what you did in thet ambush. Mighty grateful, doc. Saved my bacon—'

'Forget it. I'm all finished here. Now get some sleep, Jim, and quit squawking. If you rest up you'll be all right.'

They went outside. A dark-gowned Spanish woman, her face composed, hands in her lap, was sitting on a stool by the door. Stoppard spoke to her and his instructions followed those issued by Jubal. She inclined her head in a graceful gesture that summed it all up without words, and went inside to sit by the bed. Stoppard strode out on to the porch, stuck his thumbs into his belt, rocked on his heels, sniffed, and looked off at the sky.

'How's about that breakfast we were discussing?' Jubal spoke a little tartly.

'Sure, doc, sure. Trot right over to th' bunkhouse and get your belly fed. Yes, sir. Reckon my Jim's gonna be all right.'

'Kinda like to have my guns back. And the rifle.'

'Plenty of time for that. Plenty of time.'

It was perfectly clear to Jubal that a man of the power and vicious temper of Stoppard would never normally have tolerated for a single second the kind of treatment Jubal had been handing him. The power a doctor wielded had deeper roots into a man's soul, even, than the blustering wealth and pistol-backed power of the rancher.

'Hey, doc, come and wrap yourself aroun' bacon and beans.' Hank waved from the bunkhouse door and Jubal went over.

The oldster still chawed right up to the last moment before eating. He shook his head, marvelling. 'Caught that run in with young Abe. Mighty headstrong feller he was, allus was, ever since he could holler.' He gave Jubal a straight-eyed glare. 'Ain't the same boy since—' And stopped, and scooped a tin spoonful of beans, slopping the rich sauce down his stubbled chin.

'Since he married Candice,' Jubal finished for him.

'Yep, but I ain't sayin' so.'

'And his sister? Annie?'

Hank wiped his fingers on a hunk of bread, wiped the tin bowl, popped the bread into his mouth. 'Whut yo' don't know won't harm you.'

Jubal broke off a hunk of bread, saying: 'Nice to have real bread as well as pancakes. Real civilized.'

'You mess with Annie – she's Annie Patterson now – and young Abe's missus gets to hear – you won't worry much about how civilized they are hereabouts.'

Casually, leaning back, looking through the open bunkhouse door, conscious of the emptiness of the place, for the hands had been sent off, Jubal said, 'And Jess Hawken?'

Hank let the chaw and the knife in his hands slip – almost. 'Jess? Tain't no business o' yourn.'

'I know. Just talking. He's back in town.'

'So I hear. And up to his shooting shenanigans again.'

'Forced on him.'

'He shouldn'a took to being a gunslinger, then! Annie was fair mizzled by it – cried her purty li'l eyes out—'

'She didn't give Jess any sign.'

'Course not! Annie's a lady!'

'And there was Mat Patterson, of course.'

'In course. Fine lad, fine lad. Wisht young Abe had let me ride off with the boys.'

'The bunkhouse—'

'Yeah. They's all off chasing the Croxley Boys.'

'They didn't get much sleep,' said Jubal, but whilst his mouth framed the words his brain seethed with frustration and resentment. He had to get away, and fast. The notion that some stupid hick cowpoke, or some rattler-faced gunhand, should send a slug into Lee Kincaid awoke the dormant fury in him. His face took on that thin-lipped, taut-skinned, ferocious look of animal passion. Hank rocked back.

'Jumping Jehoshaphat, doc! They's a real mean streak in you, surely.'

'Man I have to kill riding with the Croxley Boys.'

'You don't say. I'd rather kill 'em all—'

'Not this one. He's mine.'

'Young Abe won't let you off the spread 'til Jim's better.'

'Maybe.'

'Anybody special?'

'Lee Kincaid.'

Before Hank could answer, a staccato beat of gunfire blasted outside. The sounds rolled brazenly under the sun. As one, Hank and Jubal hit the floor. Not a bullet punched through the walls of the bunkhouse. The rifle fire increased to a crescendo and then gradually eased up with isolated shots cracking off and fading away to the rear of the ranch house.

Hank crawled to the door, hesitated, turned to stare back at Jubal.

Jubal said; 'It's your head.'

'Guess I'll wait awhiles. See what happens.'

Easing up alongside a window and making sure that he was not framed in the opening, Jubal looked out. By carefully moving from side to side he could cover a good view of the dusty stretch leading up to the front porch of the ranch house. A few tired shade trees grew over the well. A broken buckboard stood beyond the far well, a fresh wheel and scattered implements lying by the still body of the blacksmith. Smoke rose from his forge. His bellows had been shot through into tatters.

A belch of smoke and a crash from the ranch house window indicated that someone – probably Stoppard himself – fancied he'd spotted a target. Instantly a fusillade of carbine and rifle fire broke against the wall. Splinters of wood flew and the curtains shook like a waterfall in spring. Someone was yelling deep inside the house as the gunfire ceased.

Hank quickly withdrew his head from around the door.

'See any o' the varmints, doc?'

'There's one sheltering behind the well. Sharps. There's another up in the shade tree – Spencer. There are two Winchesters out there – not spotted 'em yet.'

'One at the far angle o' poor Ned's forge.'

Jubal squirmed around, well away from the window, getting a clear picture of the forge. He saw a sudden glint of metal.

'Got him.'

'Cain't spot the other bastard.'

'He'll let us know when he's ready.'

Hank spat neatly. 'The rest of 'em must be working some deviltry at the back. Most likely getting set to fire the place.'

'It's a thought.'

'Got my old Henry. Suppose young Abe relieved you o' yore piece?'

'Unfortunately. No guns in here?'

'Nary a one, doc. The boys took 'em after the Croxley Boys.'

'And the Croxley Boys have come avisiting. Pity they missed the gunhands Stoppard's been paying. Wasted money.'

'Waal, doc. Think I'll just mosey over to th' ranch house. See how young Abe and young Jim are making out. Most likely they'll need a little help right around now.'

'You won't make it across there, old-timer.'

'Mebbe. But it's gotta be done.'

'Just hold your horses for a spell, Hank.'

'What you figgerin', doc?'

'Suppose I run and you cover me with the Henry?'

'Not your fight.'

'True – and untrue.'

Again Hank flinched from the lethal blaze of killing anger in Jubal's face. He shifted his wad from cheek to cheek.

'You sure want that rattler Kincaid bad, doc.'

'Yes. Glad I ate breakfast. Going to be a big day ahead.'

'Slew o' fellers never going to see the sunset.'

'You figuring on Bill bringing the Hissing S riders back here on the swing trail? Following Croxley?'

'It figgers, doc. It sure do. There's mebbe fifteen, twenty o' the varmints out there now. Young Abe and young Jim and a ranch house crew — Fred and Tony and Buck-Tooth Harrison in there for sure — just gotta hold out. They need my help.'

'Listen,' Jubal said positively. 'You can be more help here with the Henry. You've got enfilade fire.'

'You're a doc. Can you do something' for that condition?' Hank looked suddenly apprehensive. 'Sounds powerful trouble.'

'It can be, for anyone who gets in the way.'

Hank took a scratch at his white stubbled jaw. 'You mean I gotta sit on my arse here and wait until they rush? Then shoot the varmints up their tails as they go by?'

'When they attack from here. You can see only a portion of the back of the house—'

'Thet's where the varmints are right now—'

'Surely. And the back of the bunkhouse is turned away from the ranch house. I'm going out through the back door, take a look around — you keep up a watch and be ready with enfilade fire.'

'Hey, doc, there's jist one flaw in your plans.' Hank's piercing eyes rolled to the back wall of the bunkhouse.

'Oh, no there's not,' said Jubal. He went to the wall, selected his spot and kicked the planking softly, testing.

Hank whistled round his chaw. 'I was gonna say there ain't no door in th' back wall o' the bunkhouse — seems I coulda kept my fool mouth shut.'

'Use the Henry when you have to, Hank. Don't waste shells — don't waste yourself.'

Hank scored a direct hit into the spittoon, his pride and joy, and Jubal eased the planking free to create an opening wide enough to slip through. Outside the bunkhouse he looked carefully in all directions. The view took in the end of a corral where a handful of horses moved uneasily between the bursts of noise, a shade tree that needed a wash and brush up, and the crest of a rise that would take a rider up through the Hissing S land out on to the trail to the Manford spread. Jubal twisted around and peered into the bunkhouse.

Hank nodded and jerked his head.

Jubal revealed his two broken front teeth in a boyish smile. Then he turned back to the sunshine and started his deadly game of hunt and kill.

Hank had figured on there being fifteen or twenty of Croxley's Boys surrounding Stoppard's ranch house. Jubal had estimated four out front so, with another three each side, that ought to leave either five or ten out back. In a crouching run he headed for the ridge where scrub and yellowed grass grew on the untended land. From there he could look across and down on the back of the house. Smoke burst from a rear window and the smash of the carbine echoed against the dry earth.

Answering fire spurted from a group of logs stacked ready for chopping. Farther on a broken-down shed with a sagging roof gave evidence of occupation by riflemen. Jubal considered.

His view gave him a good sight of the four men who rose from concealment. They kept low and headed out beyond the far wall of the house. Jubal could only watch them go. Clearly, Zeke Croxley had a scheme going and needed more men that side, or at the front. Again Jubal considered. It seemed likely to him that Croxley might try to fool Stoppard into thinking the main weight of the attack was coming in from the back, and instead switch the effort to the front. From all he had heard of Croxley, the outlaw was shrewd as well as vicious.

Keeping flat, Jubal wriggled forward and off the ridge. He eased his way through brush and came out ten yards from the log pile. The sun was building up into the fierce desolating heat of midday. Dust whirls lifted and spun and dropped out on the flat. Sweat dribbled past his eyes and nose. He eased on and then halted, getting his feet under him, drawing in deep powerful breaths.

There were three outlaws in back of the logs. Every now and then one would lift and wing a shot into the back wall of the house. Smoke hung, bitter on the hot air. Answering fire remained spasmodic. If Hank was right, and there was a three-man ranch house crew in there, they'd be thinly spread.

In a pause one of the men rolled onto his back and fished the makings from a shirt pocket. His stubbled face looked very dark in the shade.

'Guess old man Stoppard's wetting his britches by now.'

'Not him,' opined the second man, drawing cartridges from his bandolier and popping them into the Winchester 66. 'He's as hard as this ground.'

'My old Sharps will drill clean through him,' said the third, dropping the lever and releasing the breech block. He shoved a big cartridge up the breech and closed the lever with a decisive click. 'I'll drill him from arse to breakfast time.'

All three carried revolvers in raffishly-slung holsters.

Patiently, like a stalking mountain lion, Jubal waited his moment. It came as a shot raked out from the ranch-house and the Sharps man lifted and fired a snap return shot. The Winchester operator also shot, riffling off three quick ones. The other man licked his smoke and stuck it in the corner of his mouth – and then he was starting up, trying to swing his Winchester up from the dusty ground, yelling in horror.

Jubal powered forward in a series of long lethal bounds.

He hit the man smoking the cigarette, put a stomping foot hard into his throat. Blood gushed from the man's slack mouth, staining the cigarette, hissing against the glowing end.

The Sharps man yelled and tried to haul up. Jubal seized the smoker's Winchester and slammed the barrel into the Sharps man's guts, thrusting and twisting. In the same moment he ducked away, as the Winchester slammed a bullet over his head. He charged in again, low, and swung the carbine in a savage roundhouse swing. The butt thudded solidly into the side of the fellow's head. It knocked him sideways and backwards. Blood gushed from his nose and mouth. Without stopping, Jubal whirled, levered the action, and sent a .44 into the

Sharps man's head. Blood, brain, and bone splintered and sprayed across the log pile.

The look on Jubal's face froze the two left alive. They could not speak. Neither one had a scarred forehead. Jubal shot them both. He dived into cover as bullets spanged from the log pile in a desperate fusillade from the ranch house window. He lay for a few moments, panting, feeling the tremble tingle through his limbs.

Then he stripped off a bandolier and filled it with cartridges taken from the other dead man. He reloaded the Winchester 66 with practised smoothness.

Out of sight of the ranch-house window a man sprinted around the corner of the house.

'What's going on?' he yelled.

Jubal drew a bead on his midriff, checked the man's forehead, and pressed the trigger. The .44 sent the man staggering and Jubal punched another round into his guts for good measure. The outlaw collapsed, twitching, blood spouting from his belly and beginning to trickle from his mouth.

Four down – how many more to go before he tangled with Kincaid?

Jubal stripped out two of the brass Henry .44 rimfire cartridges. He pushed them neatly through the King receiver loading gate. The Winchester carried more rounds in the magazine than the Spencer and Jubal intended to make full use of them. He left the Beecher's Bible where it lay, the lever and block fallen down, as always seemed to happen to a Sharps if you turned it upside down. He needed rapid firepower now. His scowling face with the hate-filled brown eyes turned savagely towards the far end of the house and the sounds of gunfire.

Soon, he hoped, soon he would have Lee Kincaid eating dirt at the muzzle of this carbine.

The gunfire continued from the front of the house. Jubal eased along flat to the wall, the carbine held across his body, finger on the trigger, the hammer cocked. At the corner he could make out the frenzy of fire, and detected the different notes of different weapons in action.

Dropping flat he shoved his head out, around the corner, taking in the scene brilliantly etched in bright sunshine.

The old Henry was banging away from the bunkhouse door. Hank was a mere dark figure in the shadows, surrounded by a cloud of gunsmoke. Bullets ripped across the open space drilling into the ranch-house, splintering wood from around the bunkhouse door in a withering cross fire. Return fire rained down on the forge and the well. The whole area smoked with the violence of a full-scale gun battle.

Stoppard's men were shooting wildly, attempting to hold down the volume of fire striking in at them. Three men lay in pools of blood where Croxley's first charge had withered. Jubal grimaced and took a careful bead on the Spencer man in the shade tree. He fired. The bullet knocked the outlaw from his perch. With a wild cry he fell and the carbine flew up, spinning and glinting in the sunlight. His head struck the packed dirt with a solid crunch. Blood burst from his nostrils and he flopped over, wriggling. Jubal did not spare him another glance.

Shots spanged in from his right and he hunched down and swung the Winchester muzzle. The men at the side of the house had him lined up. Two of them, they thought they had him dead to rights.

Jubal cursed and squeezed the trigger, rolling away after each shot, feeling the bullets kicking dirt by his rolling body. He hit the first man and saw him rear up; his second shot missed. He rolled frenziedly again, heard a slug thump into the boards at his back with a sickening crunch, got the shooter dead centre and squeezed off. The outlaw stood. He rose from the patch of brush looking completely flabbergasted. A stain was spreading rapidly across his chest.

He stared across the short intervening space at Jubal and his hands lifted the carbine automatically.

Jubal shot him through the head, saw the gout of blood, and turned back to the gunfight out front.

A horse was galloping madly up the trail. It burst past the stockade fence and came belting crazily up through the crossfire.

The horse was a grey, lathered with foam. It leapt over the

dead bodies and skidded to a long sliding halt. The rider, swathed in a long cloak, fell off rather than dismounted.

Slugs kicked dust about the struggling horse. It let rip a terrified whinny that changed to a screaming neigh of pain as bullets hit it. The rider in the cloak staggered up. He was cradling a bundle close to his chest.

Jubal yelled.

He shouted in a bellowing, ferocious, ripping voice above the noise of gunfire.

'Hold your fire! It's a woman! Hold your fire!'

The gunfire slackened, died away.

Steadily, the figure advanced towards the stoop of the Stoppard ranch-house.

The covering hood fell away to reveal Beth's pallid face, drained of blood. Deep black smudges shadowed her eyes. She walked unsteadily, each step an enormous effort.

In her arms she carried her newly-born child.

'Abe Stoppard!' she called in a voice cracking with desperation. 'Send your son out here! I want to see Jim Stoppard. Where's Jim? I want him to see his son – I've brought his son to see his father!'

CHAPTER ELEVEN

The horror of the moment got to Jubal.

A young girl, raped, delivered of a child she detested, now walked falteringly on to confront the father of her baby, to show him what he had wrought. Beth staggered and held on, forcing her slender abused body upright, holding the child protectively.

A deep voice bellowed from the ranch-house. Abe Stoppard.

'Git away from here, you bitch. We don't want your sort on Stoppard range.'

'You're this baby's grandfather, Abe Stoppard. Why don't you acknowledge him? Where's Jim – *Where's Jim?*'

Jubal stood up. He held the Winchester in his left hand. This was nothing to do with him. This was not his business. But – but he had delivered this girl of her child. He owed her his duty as a doctor and in Jubal Cade's book that meant he owed her his duty as a fighting man – as a killer.

He started out at a dead run, crouching, expecting at any moment to feel the wicked crack of bullets past his head.

Long before he had covered half the distance Stoppard yelled again, vengeful anger making his words spit out like a striking rattler.

'You're lying, girl! My Jim don't run with the Croxley Boys! Git away from here.'

'He did and he give me this baby – your son, Jim – where is he? He's got a fine baby boy.'

A carbine spat from the shadowed stoop.

Beth lifted the baby as though to prove the baby's parentage to Stoppard.

The bullet struck her. She gasped and twisted around, then she fell, hugging the child back into her embrace for protection.

She fell helplessly, thudding onto the stony ground with a

bone-wrenching crash. Jubal drove on with quick vicious strides, diving and skidding in a cloud of dust to reach her.

He took the baby gently into his right arm, crooking his elbow. She lay on her side staring blankly at him. The bullet had entered her chest, smashing its way through – there was nothing anyone could do for Beth Patterson now.

The men reopened fire and a hail of bullets criss-crossed over the heads of the doctor and the dying girl.

Beth gasped and blood trickled weakly from her mouth.

'It was Jim. It was. He was allus wild – running with the Croxley Boys. His father – the mean old skunk – went wild about it.' Beth's eyes closed. 'Jim brought 'em to our place to hide. Good place to hole up. He did – he did it to me. I couldn't stop him.' Her breathing wheezed now and more blood spilled from her lips. She was gasping for breath, but she ground out the words as she fought the blackness that was closing in on her. 'Jim allus wanted me. But I took no notice of the no-good skunk. Made him madder'n a dawg with fleas. He had his way in the end, tho'—'

'Hush, Beth – I'll look out for the baby—'

'Ain't it dead? I'd like it dead, like me.'

'Now, Beth—'

Nobody was shooting at the girl. The blood trickled down her chin. Her breath rattled in her throat. Then came a racking spasm that convulsed her entire body. When she relaxed she was dead.

Jubal looked at her, remembering.

He remembered the scarlet of sundown on the snow mingling with the spilled crimson of blood.

He carried with him always that ghastly, shattering picture of his wife Mary, her lower face a mask of blood where her life had been blown away. Were the dark forebodings of Mary true? Was this land doomed to be forever drenched in innocent blood?

Holding the baby to him and hefting the Winchester he scuttled back into the shelter of the wall. The old Henry boomed as Hank covered him and only four bullets came anywhere near. He slid around the edge of the house and scanned the area ahead. The men he had shot sprawled in ungainly death and the hungry flies did not rise at the intrusion.

He put the baby down carefully, lapping a fold of cloth about its tiny form. Then he checked the Winchester and started for the back of the house.

Sidling along the wall, Jubal forced himself to stop trembling. He knew his face must hold that dreadful killer look. His deep-set brown eyes would be blazing from the mask of fury, the skin stretched taut over the high cheekbones, the lips thinned back into a murderous rictus of hate.

The window nearest to him opened into a long passage.

Jubal powered through in a single lunge, hitting the floor and coming up, crouched, like a wildcat. No one was in sight. He prowled to the far end looking for a door and a gunhand came running out. He saw Jubal and started to trigger his Colt.

Jubal slewed the Winchester and fired twice. Both bullets hit the gunslinger in the head. The head exploded like a chopped cabbage.

Stoppard called out: 'Whut's going on back there?'

A woman's voice, hard, hateful, cutting.

'You plumb scared to find out, Abe? Your stupid idea sending the hands out after the Croxley Boys – and they've come here after my silver! You fool!'

The rumble of voices from the room fronting the stoop was followed by the cautious opening of the door.

Jubal slid into a cross passage where the walls were decorated with Zuñi rugs and beaded work of fine quality. He headed for the door at the far end. Inside that room he had a view of the front yard. Outside the form of Beth lay still in death and in the room Charlie sprawled dead. The bullet that killed him had drilled through the bandage around his head. He would not need Jubal's stitching service.

Smoke hung in the air, so Charlie had not been dead long.

In the side wall the door leading into the main living-room stood ajar. Candice Stoppard's shrill voice cut through the air.

'No one? You sure, you fool? Why I ever married you sure beats me hollow.'

'You wanted my money and my position, Candice. Well,'

Stoppard said in his heavy voice. 'Now you got both. And if what young Beth said about Jim is true—'

''Tain't true! Can't be—' Here gunfire broke out again and drowned the words. Jubal slid across to the door. Candice Stoppard shrilled viciously at her husband. 'Why d'you think my Jim took up with the Croxley Boys in the fust place? You, of course, you spineless idiot!'

'You—'

'They made him do it! Didn't they beat him up because he wouldn't help them ambush the stage with my silver in it? Well?'

Jubal realized that, if that answered one question, it also raised a few more. Jim Stoppard, spoilt and domineering, had run away to join the Croxley Boys. He had brought them to what he considered a safe hideout after they'd hit the Larson City Bank. And there, at the Patterson place, he had raped Beth. Then Sheriff Lovesay had happened along and burned the place down. Jubal wondered how much Stoppard had paid Lovesay to keep his mouth shut.

By a half-turn of the head from his position he could look back down the passageway. The glittering barrel of a heavily engraved carbine appeared snouting past the open door. Jubal held himself taut and moved away to the inner door.

Candice Stoppard's voice shrilled on.

''Tain't no good moseying out there, Abe. Fred's got the back covered. Them Croxley scum is aiming to break in from the front – with that shameless hussy sprawled out there and all. I'll give her a good whupping crost her backside.'

Didn't the stupid bitch know poor Beth was dead, shot down in cold blood by her husband.

The engraved carbine withdrew. Jubal swung away, with a quick look through the window, and headed on down to the inner door. Then he froze.

Hoofbeats battered across the hard-packed dirt of the yard. The timber of the stockade gate broke asunder into flying shards. A pair of horses hauled an ancient buckboard through the gate, wheels smoking across the dusty ground.

Driving the rig the powerful frame of Jess Hawken hauled

up on the reins. At his side and bouncing with the pounding he was receiving from the buckboard sat young Mat, his boyish face tense with excitement, the big old Enfield rifled musket looking like a redwood pointing up past his head. The rest of the Patterson kids howled and squealed in the bed of the buckboard, the very wagon that had taken Jubal to the Patterson place to treat their pregnant sister.

Now she lay dead, killed by the father of her son's father, and the baby was crying away in the scrub down by the wall of his grandfather's luxurious ranch-house.

'Get down, Jess! Get them kids out of it!' bellowed Jubal.

The buckboard rocked to a standstill, the horses rearing and the kids tumbling off into the dust. Jess flung the reins at the horses' heads and dived off. Mat went the other way.

Kath was there, hobbling along, the tears streaming down her face. She saw Beth and screamed and tried to run. With her hip jutting awkwardly, she began to limp over to the body of her sister.

From the back of the buckboard emerged the elder sister, Izah. She held a Remington derringer, twin to the one Jubal had in keeping for her. She ran with Hawken and the kids swiftly towards the ranch-house.

Jubal leaned across the window-sill and started pumping bullets at the well, at the forge, at the betraying bursts of gun-smoke that burst from Croxley's gang.

Through the crash of gunfire Stoppard's deep voice echoed in the room.

'Keep it up, Charlie! Get them skunks! Aim at the Patterson scum!'

Jubal shot the carbine empty and began to rip out fresh shells, twisting the bandolier to get at the loads.

A slug cracked into the window frame by his head and showered splinters into the room. He ducked down and rammed the .44 Henry rimfires in through the loading gate, cursing the folly of it all. What in the blue blazing seventh hell did Jess Hawken mean by bringing kids up here? They'd all get themselves killed . . .

When he'd loaded the carbine he set himself and leaped for

the window, taking an immediate bead on a Croxley Boy who incautiously showed himelf at the near side of the well.

Jubal blew him away and stared in horror as the stream of yelling kids, waving kitchen knives and pitchforks – little Lou brandished a pair of scissors – raced for the front porch of the ranch-house. Jess Hawken was not in sight. Kath crouched weeping by the still and bloodied form of her sister. Jubal cursed again and triggered a quick shot at an outlaw who was trying to get in closer beyond the forge. The outlaw stopped running and slid to his knees. He threw his carbine away. He went on sliding, upright on his knees, the dust smoking away in a long trail. Then he fell over, kicked, and lay still, his Stetson still on his head.

He was not Kincaid.

A bunch of riders approached the stockade gate which the buckboard had smashed open. Sheriff Gil Lovesay led out, riding hard, his deputies and a few barflies and storekeepers hauling up in back of the wooden fencing. Lovesay wheeled about, a bullet cracked under his horse's nose, and he, too, pulled back and dismounted in a hurry.

'Sheriff and his posse arriving just too late as usual,' snarled Jubal. He had no time to waste on Sheriff Gil Lovesay. He saw Dolman sliding from his horse and yanking a Winchester from his boot. The town of Rawson had roused itself out to send this posse after the Croxley Boys.

Jubal shinned along to the door, hugging the side wall tight as paint. He could see through the crack and made a swift check before bursting in. He had business in that room.

Hawken was in the act of swinging around like an enraged old bull, bellowing at the kids over the gunfire from outside.

'You kids are plumb loco! Get out! Scram! Vamoose! You're like to get yourselves all kilt!'

Young Mat dived under Hawken's arm, heading for the rear.

'We made you bring us, Jess, and we're here on business.'

Stoppard and his wife over on the far side stood goggling at the avalanche of children. Their savage faces would make anyone stand back a step.

The other gunhands in the room, men Hank had mentioned, recovered from the shock first.

One of them fired at Jess Hawken. The old gun fighter merely twisted his arm and blasted a single shot. The gunsel slumped, blood running down his face from his ruined eye. He dropped his gun and buckled at the knees and collapsed. Stepping around the door, Jubal blasted the other gunhand even as Hawken shot him. The two slugs furrowed into the man's head and chest, knocking him over into a spreading torrent of his own blood.

'Jubal!'

Hawken stared across the smoke-filled room.

'Beth,' said Jubal. 'Stoppard shot Beth.'

The ornamental Winchester in Abe Stoppard's fists snouted between Hawken and Jubal. He was sweating. His heavy face showed a wild anger and despair foreign to his nature.

'Go on, you fool!' screeched Candice Stoppard. 'Shoot the no-good skunks!' She brought her own carbine up, her face twisted with fury and fear and bitter vengeance. 'Iffen you can't, I will—'

She pointed the gun directly at Hawken. The big gunfighter stood, transfixed.

'Cain't shoot a woman—' he began.

A shot blasted from the front door.

Candice Stoppard spun about, shocked, letting the Winchester fall, as a great wad of bloody flesh tore from her back. Over her right breast a dark and ominous stain flowered on the expensive dress.

Dolman stepped throught the door, a smoking Galand and Somerville self-extractor in his hand. He swivelled to blast Hawken from the back. Candice Stoppard fell to her knees cupping her ruined breast and staring down in horror at the red wetness spreading over her hand. Dolman aimed at Hawken, his thin moustache stretching over his lips in an evil smile. In the next second the hammer would fall—

Izah put her little .41 Remington Derringer into Dolman's side and fired. The bullets drilled him through. His revolver went off and the bullet ploughed harmlessly through the ceiling. Dolman's yell mingled with the hysterical blood-choked screeching of Candice Stoppard.

Abe Stoppard looked down on his wife and his face twisted in shock and revulsion. He took a step back, going in the direction Jubal had not expected him to go.

Hawken triggered a shot that splashed past Stoppard and clanged against a Cavalry sabre hung on the wall. Stoppard yelled and ran. He dived for the rear door and went on through as Jubal cut loose. Hawken fired again, but both bullets chipped wood from the architrave.

'The goddam bastard's gettin' away,' bellowed Hawken. He started for the rear door.

'He took that fancy Winchester with him, Jess.'

Both men hauled up by the door and a blast of lead screeched past from the rear. Hawken stared at Jubal.

'He shot Beth? What am I gonna tell Annie?'

The sound of gunfire from outside had now slackened. Heavy footfalls tramped on the stoop and men filled the front door. Lou danced around waving her scissors. Perce and Sam had found themselves Colts taken from the nerveless hands of dead gunslingers and it looked as though a fresh battle would flare up.

Jubal's voice rang out, cracking like a cattleman's stockwhip. 'Put those guns down, Sam! Perce! That's the Sheriff!'

'And you'd better put your gun down, too, doc,' said Sheriff Gil Lovesay, advancing into the room. Smoke wreathed in flat lazy coils over the floor. The smell of fired powder stung in the air. 'Put that gun down, doc, or I'll plug you!'

The sound of Izah sobbing made them all turn. She sat on the floor by Dolman, watching as the saloon owner died. Her face glistened with tears. Candice Stoppard was dead, her torso a red ruin.

Lovesay glared at Hawken.

'You go for your gun, Jess, you're dead as a doornail.'

'Dolman shot Candice, Gil.'

'Let's git Mr Stoppard in here. He'll sort this out.'

All Jubal's anger flared. His face took on that grotesque caricature of death. This wasn't finished yet – by hell it wasn't!

'Abe Stoppard murdered Beth Patterson, Sheriff.' Jubal spoke in an ice-cold voice that snapped Lovesay's head around.

'And I'm not putting this gun down until that rat has been arrested for murder.'

'You'd better do as the Sheriff says, doc,' put in Ray, the deputy, fidgeting nervously. 'We don't want to lose the only doc in Rawson.'

'What about the Croxley Boys?' countered Jubal. 'What happened out there?'

'They rode off when we tossed 'em a little lead—'

'Rode off!' Again Jubal wondered what business he had here. He should be out there, riding after Croxley and his gang, seeking the scar-faced killer of his wife. But the sight of Beth, dying with her baby in her arms, ghosted into his mind.

'I'm going after Stoppard. He's not getting away with murder.'

'You move, Cade, and you're dead.' Sheriff Lovesay pointed his Colt directly at Jubal's belly. His sweating face showed clearly he was longing for the chance to drive a bullet home.

'Then you'd be dead, too, Gil,' said Hawken, calmly.

The Sheriff gestured to the men at his back. 'Act yore age, Jess!' He swung to Jubal. 'I gave you fair warnin'. The last time, doc – put down that gun!'

Jubal stepped to the side wall where the door led off to the side passage. A table stood there littered with the bric-a-brac a woman like Candice would collect. Metal glittered on the table top. He faced the Sheriff and threw the Winchester onto the floor. He stood back, his arms outspread from his sides.

'That's better, doc.'

A shout and a vicious yell sounded from the back of the ranch-house.

'Whut's going on in there?' demanded the Sheriff. He bellowed towards the door, his face ugly. 'Mr Stoppard! Mr Stoppard, you there? It's th' sheriff. I got these two varmints safe, Mr Stoppard.'

'Then shoot th' bastards! Shoot 'em out of hand!' The answering yell sounded thick, as though Stoppard spoke with difficulty.

'You'd better git in here, Mr Stoppard.'

The guns of the sheriff and his deputies held on Jubal and

Hawken. The children moved to the side, huddling together, gripped in the tension of the moment. Only young Lou pranced about, trying to stick her scissors into the legs of the nearest man. He looked down. It was Hardman the storekeeper.

'Now, now, missy,' he said. 'You be careful with them things.' He bent and took the scissors away. Lou didn't cry but started kicking him in the shins. Hardman backed off, holding his rifle awkwardly and clearly at a loss.

In the tiny moment of distraction provided by Lou Abe Stoppard stepped around the door. Lou's incensed efforts were due, Jubal guessed, to ancient wrongs and indignities suffered at the hands of the storekeeper. But the distraction was enough.

Stoppard's face hung loosely. His eyes glared. He aimed the Winchester at Hawken and the kids, after taking a single quick look at the dead and bloody body of his wife.

'So you skunks shot Candice – she was a bitch and a nagger, but she was mine—'

'Dolman shot her,' said Jess Hawken. His empty hands gripped into fists and relaxed, gripped and relaxed.

'Now, Mr Stoppard—' began Sheriff Lovesay.

'Shutup, Gil.' Stoppard's eyes showed a glazed blank look that Jubal fancied indicated the man's mind had become unhinged. Perhaps not. For everything would be settled Stoppard's way, now he had the drop on them, and he would quickly get over the loss of Candice and find himself a younger and prettier wife to bed. The Hissing S spread and the town of Rawson would remain the property of Abe Stoppard.

Sparkling anger blazed in Jubal's face. He took a step back, nearer the side table with its mess of ornaments and bric-à-brac.

'You shot and murdered Beth, Stoppard,' he said, and the evil look of fury on his face glowered down on the rancher. 'Your son Jim raped Beth. Her baby's outside now, a living proof—'

'Lies! Lies!' Stoppard howled. The fancy Winchester swung away from Hawken and the Patterson children and centred on Jubal.

'Not lies, Stoppard. The Patterson family know the truth.

They know your son Jim took the Croxley Boys to their place to hide out when the going got too hot for them. They know what happened. Jim Stoppard is a rapist, and you are a murderer.'

Jubal's calculated words had the effect he desired.

Even as he finished he powered sideways. He had taken all Stoppard's maniacal attention away from the kids and Hawken. He'd directed that killing frenzy towards himself.

Stoppard's carbine flamed. The bullet snapped past Jubal and flattened against an iron bracket holding a decorated pot filled with plants. The ringing note gonged in the smoke-shrouded room. Jubal lunged for the side table. Stoppard's second bullet chopped a photograph into splinters. Jubal dived.

The third bullet caromed off a brass urn on the table and then Jubal had his Spencer in his hands. He went on with his dive, rolling over, kicking to come up into a crouch.

The lever of the old Spencer operated with that oiled sliding crisp action and a round pumped up into the breech from the butt stock. Jubal touched off the trigger.

Stoppard froze.

He stood, upright, gasping, the carbine a useless hunk of wood and metal in his hands. He lifted his arms and the gun dropped from nerveless fingers. He stood, his eyes wide with shock. Over his heart a small round hole showed black, with a little dribble of blood staining the fancy silk vest.

He took a single unsteady step, and as though the movement broke something deep within him, a great flowering gush of crimson blood spurted from his chest. He crashed over on to his face, his legs shivered in a spasm of unco-ordinated kicking, then he straightened out, stiff as a doorpost.

'Guess Stoppard never did have enough heart for a big man,' said Jubal.

The Spencer moved its muzzle towards the Sheriff and his deputies. It was not needed. In the hands of Sam and Zack and Perce the guns looked ridiculously big. But they were held firmly and they covered the group with the Sheriff.

Jess Hawken bent and retrieved his revolvers. He looked at Sheriff Lovesay, and his weather-beaten old face crinkled with pleasure.

'Stoppard was gonna cut us down, Gil. He was gonna kill us in cold blood, like he kilt poor Beth. And you, you bastard, would have done nuthin' – just as you did nuthin' about Jim and Beth – 'cause you knew, Gil. You knew.'

Lovesay looked shattered. Sweat caked on his forehead and glistened on his cheeks.

'Yeah, I knew. I knew, Jess. But what could I do? Stoppard is a big man in these parts – my job—'

'*Was* a big man, Gil.'

'Yeah. Guess so.'

From the back area came the sounds of a yell, fierce and exultant, and the crack of a Colt. Everyone swung to look through the rear door except Jubal. He kept the Spencer centred on the Sheriff. The Colt bellowed again and then there echoed the deep-voiced thump of an old rifle musket going off.

'Mat!' said Hawken, taking a step towards the door.

Smoke billowed around the frame. A shadow darkened the doorway. Jim Stoppard appeared, a smoking Colt revolver in his hand. He was smiling. His ravaged face looked bland with the smile. He coughed. Blood welled up from his insides and ran out over his teeth and lips. The crimson tide splashed down his chin and ran on to his chest. He sagged to his knees, toppled, fell all asprawl.

Before anyone could move, Mat Patterson stepped through.

Blood stained his left cheek where a bullet had ploughed through the skin. He held the old Enfield. Smoke drifted from the upturned muzzle. He stood over Jim Stoppard, looking down, and his face reminded Jubal of the face he sometimes saw in the mirror.

'Guess Beth is paid for now, Jim,' said Mat.

He looked down, leaning on the Enfield. Then he kicked Jim Stoppard in the side. Once. Just one kick that expressed his feelings. But Jim Stoppard did not feel the kick. He had gone to join his father and mother in that place reserved for the privileged rich who care nothing for anyone on this earth but themselves and their own gratifications.

Jubal moved to the door. He moved purposefully. In the

uncanny silence after the last action everyone turned to stare uncomprehendingly at the slim form of the doctor.

Jess Hawken recovered first.

'Where you going, Jubal?'

'Outside. I'm going to fetch Beth's baby. I think the new owner of the Hissing S will need some attention.'

CHAPTER TWELVE

They brought Annie Patterson's rocking chair out on to the stoop of the ranch-house of the Hissing S spread so she could be with the others when they bid farewell to Doctor Jubal Cade. Annie Patterson sat as erect as ever with much of the bitter twist to her lips relaxed. At her side stood Jess Hawken, still big and burly, and his hand rested on Annie's shoulder. She put up her own hand, and touched his, and from time to time she would look up into his face, and smile.

All the Patterson kids were there – Zack and Sam and Perce and Lou. Kath stood with the baby in her arms, and her face showed a sweet tenderness as she cradled the small body.

The Stoppard ramrod, Bill, and the other gunhands had elected to take their due wages and ride on. Hawken expressed himself as plumb pleased they were taking off. Wouldn't be trouble, he said, to hire new men who were punchers first and gunslingers a long ways after. The troubles with Rawson should be over – until, as everyone knew, the next bunch of redskins decided to break off the reservation.

Jubal sat the fine strong grey they'd given him, a mount he'd chosen from the Hissing S remuda and cut out, personally. He sat there in the sunlight resplendent in his brand new dark grey suit, with the lighter grey vest, his pants marvels of perfection. He looked a real city dude. His old suit was carefully packed away in his saddle bags, beautifully cleaned and repaired and pressed by Mrs Patterson and Kath. A fine new white shirt shone brilliantly under the vest, and the black boot string tie was knotted in meticulous fashion. He looked very fine, did Jubal Cade, sitting his new horse.

Only the battered old grey derby tended to detract from the impression he created. Hardman carried a line of derbies; but most were brown and not a one of them had anything like the distinction of style Jubal's English-made derby betrayed in every curve.

'Mr Smith shore did you proud, Jubal,' opined Jess Hawken, his hand on Annie Patterson's shoulder.

'Feel a real dude.'

'You shore you gotta leave?'

'Sure. Fellow I have an appointment with is out there with the Croxley Boys.'

Hank came shuffling across the yard, chewing away, expertly impaling a fly on the wing with a single cheek-bulging squirt.

'Hey, doc,' he said, looking up and squinting against the brilliant sunshine. He carried a square mahogany box. 'Young Abe was mighty headstrong, and I guess now he's gone I can breathe a little easier. He allus said he'd leave me these in case he was tooken fust.' He held the box up to Jubal. 'Reckon they ain't no good to me. Sorta might come in handy where you're going, partiklar as they took your Colt and it ain't showed up.'

Puzzled, Jubal took the box. It was heavy. He balanced it and opened the lid. He whistled.

Two Beaumont-Adams revolvers nestled in their compartments in the red velvet-lined box. With them came the usual accessories – all adapted to .44 Winchester Centre Fire. The magnificence of the gift affected Jubal.

'But – Hank—'

'Still got my old Henry. Never could git the hang o' a itsy-bitsy handgun. Take 'em, doc, and put em to good use.'

'I'll do that, Hank.'

Izah Patterson stood with her family though a tiny gap still separated them. They had accepted her back, the stigma of her profession as a saloon girl having been pushed into the background in the light of the greater recent happenings. Now she gave Jubal a smile, her face already mending, and he figured she would soon be fully recovered. Then there'd be a steady procession of eligible young men riding up to the stoop of the Patterson spread – as it would no doubt be called. One thing for sure, Jess Hawken had already begun changing the Hissing S brand to the Prancing P.

'If that Arnie Javaro comes a-moseying around here lookin' for you, Jubal, reckon I'll git him to taste a little lead.'

'Now don't you go gitting into any more gun fights, Jess!' warned Annie Patterson. 'If we're to be married reckon I want a husband I can count on coming home at nights.'

'Sure thing, Annie. I'll let Gil take care of it.'

Jubal laughed and closed the lid of the box. He stowed it carefully away in the saddlebag, and gave a push to make sure his valise was securely strapped. At the same time, as a reflex action, his hand stroked along the butt of the Spencer. The two went hand in hand in his life.

Jubal heeled the grey out across the yard and let her walk for a space, enjoying the easy motion of that powerful grey body. He turned in the saddle and looked back at the group watching him ride off.

He took off his grey derby and raised it over his head.

'So long,' he called. 'Maybe, one day, I'll take a swing back through Rawson.'

'So long, Jubal. So long, doc.' Their farewells echoed after him as he rode out on to the dusty trail that drew him on to a destiny he could not avoid. 'Look to see you ridin' back some day.'

Dust puffed under the grey's hooves. Jubal jammed the old grey derby back on his head with an air of purpose.

'So long, Jubal!' they called after him.

Ahead of him the trail lay dusty and beckoning, smoky in the heat, leading on over the ridge to the far horizon.

145 70574